EVIL REIGN

Kaelin C. Murphy

EVIL REIGN

Edited by S. B. Goodman and S. L. Hoffman

Cover graphic art by Alexey Stiop used by permission granted by license from veer.com.

Title graphic font created by Cooltext.com which grants unlimited usage.

Published by Fleek Books, 2014

Printed in the United States of America

ISBN: 978-0-9960462-0-6

Dedication

For my brother, Rod, who probably doesn't realize that it was his enthusiasm that fanned the flame I had within me to write.

Though many years have passed, I can still see his face as he lay across my bed listening to me read a portion of a story I was writing. Each day when I had finished reading to him he would beg me to write more so that he could find out what happened next.

The story stayed alive and grew for many years. It evolved until it was not only a part of our lives, but took on a life of its own.

This is that story.

Acknowledgements

A belated thank you is owed to my eighth grade teacher, Mr. Coffin, who took me aside after class to confess he had taken stories I had written to the school board members who agreed with him that I should consider a career as a writer. I laughed, of course, I wanted to be the greatest surgeon that ever lived.

Thanks to Mrs. Smith, my English teacher, a little woman in Richmond Maine with a strong voice who instilled in me the power of words.

And to my daughter, Sharon, for giving me the opportunity to visit Salem, Massachusetts and to soak up its history of witchcraft and the occult. Thanks for believing in me and never letting me give up.

To my best friend, Sallye, who always finds ways to encourage me, never letting me get away with being negative. I know at times I'm a piece of work, but she never gives up on me.

And last, but in no way the least, thanks to Mom and Dad, for always believing I could do this. I wish you were both still here, so that I could place this book in your hands.

EVIL REIGN

Kaelin C. Murphy

FLEEK
Books

*But pray ye that your flight be not in winter,
neither on the Sabbath day: For then shall be great
tribulation, such as was not since the beginning of
the world to this time, no, nor ever shall be.*

St. Matthew 24:20

CHAPTER 1 – THE SABBAT

The thunder of horses' hooves and the snap of twigs and boughs, broke the silence of midnight, and announced the arrival of Satan's faithful. The horses and their evil riders emerged from the shadows of the tall New England pines, and stomped into a field, glittering with crusty snow. A chill had come with the rising of the full moon, and the air was crisp. The horses had been driven hard, and were glossy with sweat and their manes were speckled with white frothy spittle. Nervously, they pranced in place while their nostrils blew out clouds of vapor that hung eerily in the still air of the valley.

It was the Festival of Winter, February 2, 1692, and the Witches' Sabbath–or Sabbat as it was called by the faithful–would soon begin. Loyal coven members had traveled hundreds of miles to Salem Village to take part in the Festival, bringing with them their initiates and grotesque familiars. The last horse bolted from the thicket of pines, the whites of its eyes bulged with terror. Its rider wasn't human. It was an amalgam of demons from Hell. This familiar was the attendant to the High Priestess, a gift from the Master to the most powerful witch attending the Festival.

The vile creature was the size of a small child, but that was where the resemblance ended. Its thick, muscular legs–miss-shaped by the bulging veins that twisted and turned just beneath the skin–were a vice around the horses' middle.

Talons on the ends of its long, scrawny fingers were buried deep in the animal's flesh. The demon dropped its lower jaw and its mouth hung open from ear to ear, exposing sharp, jagged teeth. It let out a laugh not unlike a hyena, then sunk its long fangs into the left side of the horse's neck. The horse's lips quivered high above its teeth as it let out a shrilly neigh that was cut off abruptly as blood filled the horse's throat. The demon ripped away a large chunk of flesh, and sat upright with it clenched in its teeth. Blood gushed from the horse's wound and spattered crimson on the snow. The demonic imp shivered at the sight of it, threw back its head, and swallowed the warm, raw meat, letting out yet another fiendish laugh. Then it leaped from the horse's back and landed solid on its feet. A humpback prevented it from standing erect as it scampered on bowlegs across the field to where the faithful stood waiting for the ceremony to begin.

The initiates–not yet accepted into the circle of evil–were dressed in brown robes and sacks had been placed over their heads to prevent them from looking upon the faithful. Whimpers could be heard among them as some realized their upcoming fate. Their trembling hands clutched tightly to their copy of the gospels that would soon be forsaken before all.

Many of the flock lit black candles made of human tallow. An acidulous, putrid odor filled the air as hundreds of candles blazed, creating a large circle of light in the center of the field. Within reach of its glow, the faithful sat in the snow, oblivious to the cold. They opened their robes and invited their familiars to bite their flesh and to suck their blood.

From the mass of black robed figures, one stepped forward. The murmur among the flock fell silent as he walked to the center of the lighted circle of fire. He stopped in front of the High Priestess' attendant, and spoke with a voice that rumbled through the night like the deepest note on a violincello.

"Cleobis," the man called the familiar by his name, "we were summoned here by the High Priestess. Why has she not joined us?"

Cleobis lifted a bony finger and pointed to a hill. There, a solitary form in a black hooded robe stood facing Salem Harbor. The imp's face twisted into an insane grin as long strands of bloody drool hung from the corners of its smile. As it answered, its yellow eyes flashed with excitement that could barely be contained, and a low, demented laugh escaped from its throat as it said, "She speaks ... with the Master!"

***

Mary Deven stood above the flock with her black robe and raven hair blowing in the gentle breeze that came from the ocean. Beneath her robe, her body glistened with an ointment that had given her the power of flight. She opened her arms and welcomed in the moonlight, and darkness embraced her. She could feel its breath against her ear as it whispered, *"Mary, Mary."*

Satan had spoken to her many times in her sleep, preparing her for this night. He promised this Sabbat would be different from all others, and a quiver shot through her as an uncontrollable squeal spilled out into the night when she thought of the rituals to come; of what he may have planned for his faithful, and of what he may ask of her. He had asked things of her before. Things to prove her loyalty, and she never disappointed him. She had brought to him more souls and sacrifices than any other servant. Her reward was power and beauty, and for that she would forever serve him well.

Mary looked down on the sleeping, Puritan Village with disgust. "Salem, the new city of peace," she scoffed. "Rest well, for soon ye shall have no peace." She tilted back her head and laughed, but her laughter was cut short when her sharp, green eyes caught a glimpse of a figure weaving through the dense alders at the foot of the hill. She playfully watched the dark form slowly creep upon the faithful. Curiosity seemed to outweigh the safety of the trees, for the figure stepped out of the shadows to get a better look at the assembly of worshipers.

It was Ziea. A West Indian slave girl from the village. Mary had seen her before and had considered her harmless, but somehow, tonight seemed different. Tonight, the sight of Ziea made Mary yearn for the taste of blood. She toyed with the idea of using her for a sacrifice, but the voice of the Master came like thunder to her mind: *"NO!"*

A certainty trembled up and out of the earth and shook her to the core. She knew the Master well. He had other plans for Ziea. A smile crossed her lips as she listened to a voice that only she could hear. It rode on the wind and caressed her smooth, young skin with its breath.

"Mary, Mary," the voice whispered, *"tell the faithful that I will attend the Sabbat."*

Mary was paralyzed by the revelation. She heard her throat close like the slamming shut of a book, as her tongue pressed hard against the roof of her mouth. She struggled to swallow, trying desperately to push down the joy that welled up inside her. At last! She would pay homage to him in the flesh. Then as quickly as he had come to her, the wind was pulled back by the sea, and the presence of the Master left her. The vacuum of his departure sucked the very breath from her lungs, and her belly ached as she struggled to draw in the cold, night air. She then fastened her robe and started down the hillside. Her bare feet broke through the thin crust of snow, but she felt no sting from the cold, for Hell had warmed her.

One by one the faithful saw her and quieted their chatter, until the only sound to travel on the night air was the crackle of snow as she approached them. She could feel all of their eyes upon her as she walked to the center of the candle-lit circle.

Cleobis squatted on the ground behind her and slid a scrawny hand under the hem of her robe. She felt its bony fingers caress her thigh, then rake its sharp claws across her skin. The warm blood ran down her leg and the thirsty tongue of her servant fed upon it. Mary closed her eyes briefly and savored the pleasure she always experienced when feeding her familiar.

"Enough, Cleobis!" she said sharply. The imp came

out from under her robe, its face coated with her blood, and sat at the edge of the circle, licking the bloody flesh from under its talons.

Mary lifted her arms as if trying to embrace the multitude. "Listen to me, all of you that have traveled so far, thy journey was not in vain, for that which ye shall witness this night shall forever be remembered."

"Tell us what is to happen, Priestess," a voice pleaded from the horde.

"Yes," Cleobis agreed, then added with his gravelly voice, "Thou must tell them, Priestess. Thou must."

Mary reached out to the darkness and the folds of her robe opened like the wings of a huge bird in flight. She opened her mouth to speak and the words came with a force that was not her own. From the darkest depths of her soul her revelation spilled out into the night and resounded throughout the valley.

"He–will–join–us!" She beamed. Mary listened to the faithful's simultaneous gasp and relished their whispers of utter amazement. She knew her flock well. They would want to celebrate his coming. So she bent over and drew a pentagram in the snow. Stepping back, she waved her arms over the five pointed star, and the snow and ice beneath it melted away as the talismanic symbol became a flaming brand in the center of the field. The faithful formed a circle around the pentagram, and Mary led the chant.

Her voice first began as a vibration she could feel deep in her throat, and it magnified in volume until it became a steady hum that shook the bellies of the faithful and readied them for worship. Their voices joined hers and became a rhythmic hum that soon formed words of praise for the Master and beckoned his arrival. Some were overcome by the intensity of their bidding, falling to the ground and mumbling incoherently, while others stood steadfast in their worship, their voices blending to create a powerful baritone that seemed to resonate from the very center of the earth. The High Priestess was the first to feel the Master coming. Her heart beat with each footstep.

"Silence!" she demanded. All but one sound was stilled.

"Hoof-beats," an initiate whispered. "Could it be a late worshiper?"

"No," Cleobis growled. "It is the Master."

"Listen," Mary hissed at him.

Not one made a sound, and all could hear, the hoof-beats that neared them were not of a horse. It was the Beast. He walked on two legs, and the ground pulsed with his stride. All his faithful stood staring into the blackest shadows of the forest, yearning for their first glimpse of him, when out of the darkness two fire-filled eyes appeared with the pupils glowing like embers. Then he stepped into the moonlight, and all could see his form.

He was Baphomet, the Black Goat, and his name was Satan. He stood erect on two muscular legs with his split-toed hooves planted firmly on the frozen ground. His bare chest was that of a man, and around his waist he wore a red sash that covered his genitals. Two snakes, intertwined, emerged from under the sash with their tongues locked in a deadly kiss. Protruding from his back were a huge pair of wings that stirred up a wind as they opened and closed. His head was that of a ram, and a lit candle was placed between his horns. He tilted back his head and roared, and the ground beneath the faithful trembled with the eruption of his voice.

All, except Mary, fell to their knees and pressed their faces to the ground. But Mary was exhilarated at the sight of him. She would prove her loyalty by paying obeisance to him in true infernal fashion–backwards. She moved around behind him, with her back to him at all times. As she neared him she could feel the heat from his body. At the last moment, she turned, bent, and kissed his fundament. Dizzy from his scent, she opened her eyes and found him not to have a normal posterior–but a face there. The eyelids in the face slowly opened, and Mary could see the yellow glow of its eyes. Its mouth began to speak in a low, soothing tone, and she was transfixed by the seducing effect of its voice as it said, "Mary, Mary. You have been chosen."

A bolt of electricity shot through her! Her eyelids fluttered as her eyes rolled over white. The Beast turned and faced her. With two massive hands he reached for her face and pulled her to him. His forked tongue slithered out of his mouth and licked the underside of her eyelids, breaking the thin skin with his brand. He released her and she fell to the ground, writhing from his touch. From under his sash he removed his Black Book. In it were written the names of his chosen few. He touched the end of his finger to his tongue, still dripping with her blood, and with it wrote her name in the book.

"Come to me all ye that labor and are heavy laden," mocked the Beast, "and I will give you–power." The Beast was amused at his own irreverence, and his laughter filled the valley.

Mary pulled herself up from the ground and

stood, still reeling from the Master's touch. "Bring the initiates," she ordered.

The faithful stood, and the crowd parted to give the initiates a straight path to the Master. Cleobis pulled the sack off the first initiate in line, and she stood, paralyzed, at the sight of the Beast.

"Say your piece, witch," Mary demanded.

The girl, a scrawny blonde, barely fourteen, placed her copy of the gospels at the Master's feet, renouncing the Christian faith and baptism. "I deny God," her voice quivered, "the blessed virgin, the saints, father, mother, heaven, earth, and all that is the world."

"Doth thou vow fealty to him and to him only?" Mary asked.

The girl took a deep breath, and let her eyelids slowly close as she exhaled her answer. "My life for him."

Satan was pleased. He reached out a long arm and grasped the neckline of the initiate's robe. With one ferocious yank he ripped it from her body and she stood before him naked. His long, sharp nails pulsed in anticipation of leaving his mark on such a willing servant. He could savor the thrill of it no longer and raked his clawed hand across the young girl's belly, spilling her blood in the snow.

One after another came to him, each renouncing God and all that was good. He marked them all in secret places and wrote their names in his book with their blood. The faithful robed each new member in black once they had received the mark of the Beast, then the Festival began.

All who had acquired familiars, bent and kissed

their backsides–an act regarded as the ultimate abasement. All but Mary. She stood calmly in the center of the growing hysteria, admiring the Master. She would bow to no one but him ever again. Her heart pounded as if trying to fight its way out of her chest and she had to remind herself to breathe while in his presence. She saw glee in his eyes as he watched the faithful celebrate his attendance, and she knew she had done well.

The field, once a white sheet, free from sin, was now covered in blackness. It undulated with evil as the faithful unleashed their inhibitions and gave in to their every desire. Their joined bodies squirmed upon the frozen ground, praising him with vulgar, perverted acts of sex.

Mary extended an arm and waved it over the legion. "All of them," she smiled, "I give to thee." Her eyes, once bloodied as a result of his brand, again glowed a bright green and were filled with worship.

"And what of thyself?" Satan asked her. His voice was soft and deep.

"All," Mary answered without hesitation. "I give to thee–all."

The gargantuan wings on the back of the beast opened with a great noise, and the fiesta came to an abrupt halt. The multitude stood before him, awaiting his command, and the Beast threw back his horned head and roared like a lion, filling the minds of his servants with his instruction. The faithful became as one mind, as they silently moved to the outer edges of the field, forming a huge circle. More and more circles were formed, one inside the other, until the final circle–consisting of the eleven members of Mary's coven–surrounded Mary and the Beast.

The inner circle joined hands and began to dance counterclockwise. Each circle in turn danced in the opposite direction of the circle before them, until the entire field full of worshipers moved like the gears in a clock. The chant began slowly at first, then increased in tempo as the faithful danced wildly around Mary and the Beast. The Great Rite had begun.

Mary stood beside her Master and was disrobed by a sudden blast of wind from his nostrils. She fell to the ground, squirming like a snake at the foot of the Beast. She could feel the thud of his hooves as he positioned himself over her, then the merciless penetration of her virginity.

The Beast opened his mouth and all of Hell lauded the planting of his seed. The faithful ended their frenetic dance and fell to the ground, shrieking with the satisfaction of the release of a tremendous power. Mary convulsed beneath the Beast, her green eyes now a milky white. Her once smooth skin was now dry and wrinkled, and her hair had gone completely gray. The Beast backed away and she stood, held out her arms and her robe wrapped itself around her at her command.

"It is done," she said.

The faithful, with the exception of Mary and her coven, mounted their steeds and returned to the blackness of the forest, forever to dwell under its cover. Cleobis rode into the darkness on the finest of the herd, leaving his wounded horse to die in the field. Satan bent down and with a long, sharp claw protruding from the end of a finger, drew a map on the ground.

"Thou must take your coven and flee this place," he warned Mary, "for in the village below are Christians that seek your destruction. Thou must protect the offspring."

"I shall," she promised.

Suddenly a twig snapped at the foot of the hill and pounding footsteps faded in the distance.

"Ziea!" the eldest of Mary's coven cried out. "Stop her at once!"

"No! Let her go," the Beast commanded. "The righteous peasants will think her to be a witch and you'll escape the trials that are soon to come."

"Thy will be done," the eldest replied, bowing her head to him.

The Beast spread its wings and with the force of a great tornado, was caught up in the darkness, leaving Mary and her coven standing alone in the field. Mary turned her back to them and stared into the black night, her eyes a pair of glossy white moons caught in a net of wrinkles. She reached up with a clawed hand and touched the deep lines in her face, aware for the first time of the change in her appearance. She smiled and let out an insane laugh that was only a whisper. Her beauty meant nothing to her now. He had done more than change her body. He had awakened her, and she would never rest again.

With her back still to her coven she could see them huddled around the map at their feet. The corners of her mouth curled into a smile as she discovered her new power of sight. She felt she would explode if she didn't scream out into the night her appreciation of her new found gift from the Master. But she kept silent. She would explore this new gift and learn to use it masterfully. After all, that was what he expected of her. There would be plenty of time to tell the others. She looked upon them again in her mind's eye. They seemed lost without her. She turned and faced them and they were immediately aware of her attention. They stood and stepped back as she approached them.

"My sheep, be not afraid of my transformation. It is truly wondrous," she beamed, caressing her belly in a circular motion with a clawed hand.

"Indeed, Priestess," the eldest agreed. "Just look at what the "Lord" hath done," she mocked, and reached out to touch Mary's belly.

"Althea speaks true," a tall, thin woman named Eanna spoke out. "He hath made thee whole."

"His will be done," the coven spoke in unison.

"Yes. His will. We must leave at once," Mary told them, reminding them of Satan's warning. Again, simultaneously, they replied, nodding their heads in agreement, and followed Mary from the field.

She led them northeast, staying close to the shoreline as Satan had instructed them with the map. They traveled under the cover of darkness, resting by day in hidden cavities of the earth to escape the witch hunt. Mary never slept. She sat and meditated during each rest period, and she was learning to travel within her mind. She had been back to Salem several times since departing with her coven, and the trials had begun as the Master had foretold.

On one occasion her astral body stood at the foot of Ziea's straw bed and watched her write down on a scroll what she had witnessed at the Sabbat: The sacred Black Book, the Great Rite, and the map on the ground that told of the coven's destination. After Ziea had finished writing what she had seen, she feared the writings would be misinterpreted and she would be labeled a witch and be condemned to death, so she ran out into the field and buried the scroll.

Mary also visited the dungeons where all those accused of witchcraft were imprisoned. She walked the narrow dark halls of the jail and listened to the cries of the prisoners. The poorest stood in cells too small to allow them to lay down. Their slightly bent knees pressed hard against the walls of the cells as their slumped bodies tried to get some rest. Some died in wait of their judgment. Others made the walk to Gallows Hill and after their execution the bills for their keep–and hanging–were sent to their relatives. There on the premises Mary watched a man named Giles being crushed to death beneath a mountain of stones. He, too, was innocent.

On her last visit to the village, Mary listened as Ziea made the mistake of telling her cousin, Tituba, what she had seen at the Sabbat. Tituba, being the story teller that she was, could not keep silent and she retold the story. She was immediately imprisoned, and during severe torture, blurted the name of Ziea.

In her mind's eye, Mary watched the villagers hunt Ziea down like an animal. They scored her above the breath, tearing the flesh from her forehead, mouth, and nose until her face was bloodied. Ziea ran through the streets of Salem begging for help, but the villagers turned their backs on her as she passed, for fear the devil in her would leap into them. Ziea's river of life flowed freely from her, until weakened, she fell to the ground, her struggle for life ending with her face lying in a red pool.

Back in the physical world, Mary was discovering another gift. She could hear the thoughts of her coven:

Althea was amazed at how fast the pregnancy was progressing, and wondered if they would reach their destination before the birth. Eanna felt threatened by the offspring. Althea–being the oldest–would soon pass, and Eanna was to assume the duties of the eldest. She feared the seed of Satan would take from her this great honor. And the minds of the others were filled with doubt, for their journey had been long, and they were tired.

Mary knew it was time to tell her coven of her gifts, and of what had transpired in Salem. They were resting on a blanket of pine needles, staying within the shadows of the trees. The sun was low in the sky and soon they would venture out into the night and complete their journey.

"Come," Mary beckoned them out into the fading light. "Fear not, for I am with thee," she quipped.

One by one they came out from under the low hanging limbs of the trees and stood behind her. Mary watched them in her mind's eye. They were scowling at one another, and she knew they were puzzled as to why she had called them out while it was still light.

"Thou shalt not find the answers you seek in the face of another," she said, keeping her back to them. Althea's jaw dropped in amazement. "And close thy mouth, Althea, for it is true, I have my sight."

She turned and faced them, her eyes like orbs of light against a reddening sky. She spoke the Master's tongue and her body levitated and was immediately transported within inches of Althea's face. She looked into the eyes of the eldest and smiled.

"Fear not, Althea, we will reach the end of our journey before the birth."

Mary saw a gleam come to Althea's eyes as she realized Mary's gift of knowledge.

There was a loud noise, like the slamming shut of a door, then a flash of purple light. In that instant, Mary was standing in front of Eanna.

"No honor shall be taken from you, Eanna. Thy path has already been chosen." Eanna bowed with respect for Mary's new powers, and took several steps backward.

Furiously, Mary turned to the others. "Oh ye of little faith, I tire of your doubtful minds."

Their eyes fell from Mary's gaze, ashamed of their mistrust. "Forgive us, Priestess," they begged, dropping to their knees.

Mary could not hear them. Her eyes closed as she witnessed a vision only she could see, and listened to a voice only she could hear. Her eyes flashed open.

"We must be on our way," she quickly told them. "There is a man who comes this way by the name of Burrows. George Burrows. He was the pastor to the Christians of Salem, but as of late has been accused of being the wizard of all witches. The puritans seek his capture and come in our direction. We must hurry away from here."

There was no longer any doubt in the minds of her coven as they bid her to lead them to a safe haven. They moved silently away from the pines with their black hooded robes silhouetted in the sunset, and wove through the deep crevasses in the rocky coastline until the tide came in and forced them back upon the high ledges.

The eldest grew weary and fell behind, calling out to her leader. Mary bid the others to wait as she walked back to where Althea sat on a slanted ledge with her arms resting on her knees. She looked pale.

"Forgive my poor vision, Priestess," Althea wheezed, "I see not what you see, I know not what you know, and I do trust your judgment, my beloved, but must we continue at this pace?"

Mary moved a step closer to Althea and placed a hand on her shoulder. With her face exposed to the blackening sky, she journeyed to a place beyond human sight. She stayed silent for a few moments then a smile came to her lips, and she patted Althea on the back. "Fear not, Althea, those that would do us harm have captured Burrows and are returning him to Salem."

"Very well, Priestess." Althea closed her eyes and sighed. "I shall rest but a little more, then I shall be ready to go on."

"Rest as long as thy will, my dear," Mary whispered. She lifted her hand and pointed to a small stone house nestled back in a thicket of pine trees. "We have already completed our journey."

Althea's eyes popped open, and she wrestled to get to her feet, gazing upon the dwelling. "There will be time to rest in the shelter," she insisted.

"Not with haste," Mary snapped. She grabbed Althea's arm as she tried to pass. "We are not alone."

These few words would have once caused apprehension, but no longer. Mary could feel the excitement swell in her coven, for their bellies were hungry and they thirsted for fresh blood. Without hesitation they followed Mary through the dense brush and came out into a partial clearing in front of the stone shelter.

"Wait here," Mary told them. She neared the front door and it began to rattle on its hinges from the mere power of her mind. Inside, she could hear her prey scrambling for his weapons, and she was amused by his effort.

"Who goes there?" the man shouted from behind the door. "Be off with you, lest ye wish to be maimed."

Mary's eyes turned bloody with anger as she shook the door again. The hinges twisted from the force of her power and the door came to rest at an odd angle. Inside the hunter cursed, and within his anger found the courage to step out of the shelter.

He stood, face to face, with Mary Deven, and with a swiftness that was but a blur, she reached out with a clawed hand and raked her sharp talons across his jugular. He stumbled backward as blood gushed from the wound, and Mary and her coven were on him at once, feasting on his, still twitching, body.

Her hunger now a thing of the past, Mary stood looking down on her prey. The front of her robe was shiny with the hunter's blood as she caressed her swollen belly, knowing the time of the birth was growing near. She entered the stone shelter and walked across the hardwood floor of the tiny room. She laid down on the hunter's cot. Then–the pains came.

Althea was immediately aware of the High Priestess' condition, and came to Mary's side at once. "I am here, Priestess," she assured Mary, brushing her gray hair off her forehead with a blood smeared hand.

"It is time," she said. "Did I not tell thee we would

reach the destination before the birth?" Mary screamed with pain.

"Yes," Althea replied, and quickly moved to the foot of the cot. Her face turned pale when she lifted Mary's robe. "It comes feet first!"

"Help her, lest she die," Eanna pleaded.

"No! She will not!" Althea screamed at Eanna.

"The fetus must be turned within her before the birth," Eanna cried out, "or it will surely die!"

"There is no time," Althea growled through clenched teeth at Eanna and stared her into silence. "Leave me to do what I must."

Althea's shaky hand reached into Mary and guided the feet of the baby out of the womb. She then positioned her hand beneath the baby's torso and pulled the infant from its mother.

"It is a she," Althea announced, and laid the newborn babe on Mary's stomach.

Mary placed her two withered hands under the infant and lifted it as high as she could above her body. "Master," she whispered, "to thee I give this offering."

Thunder boomed in the heavens, and suddenly the Beast appeared, and evil was with him. He reached out and–with the swipe of a clawed hand–cut the umbilical cord, and snatched up the newborn babe. He exhaled a cloud of brimstone gas into the nostrils of the infant and said, "Thou shall be called Sarah."

The Beast bent down and placed the baby in Mary's arms, and she cradled it with a mother's love as it looked at her with yellow eyes that knew her well. Satan stroked the forehead of the newborn babe as it sucked at its mother's breast, and his eyes gleamed when he saw the tinge of red leak from the corners of the baby's lips.

His fiery eyes lifted to engage Mary's faithful gaze. "To you, Mary, I entrust my seed."

Drink waters out of thine own cistern, and running waters out of thine own well.

Proverbs 5:15

CHAPTER 2—"Take eat: this is my body..."

Twelve years had passed since the birth of Sarah, and Althea grew old and weak. She lay on the dirt floor in a dugout room beneath the stone shelter, her life slipping away. She no longer ventured out into the night with the others, she only lay in the pit, waiting for death to come. A sour stench grew in the dugout, and the others in the coven watched over her like vultures waiting for their prey to ripen.

Mary provided food only for Sarah, leaving the others to feed themselves. They lived off the wildlife in the area: deer, beaver, muskrat, and at times rodents and the plentiful milk adder snakes that burrowed into the pit. During the winter months there were times when they were unable to leave the dugout to find food, and it was then that Mary fed Sarah as she had fed her familiar, allowing her to suck her life's blood until she had her fill.

The others resorted to a lottery. The loser choosing the part of their body to be dismembered for food.

Mary developed sores where she had fed Sarah. They were wounds that wouldn't heal, and they oozed yellow puss and smelled of rotting flesh. Sarah seemed not to mind. She gorged herself on Mary's life's blood at every opportunity, lifting her face periodically to gaze at Mary with a pair of glowing, yellow eyes that reminded Mary of the Master and gave her strength to go on.

Eanna approached her leader with hesitation. "Priestess, might we venture out into the night in search for food? We've not heard nor seen any by passers for weeks now. Surely it would be safe. We could be back here before the dawn."

Mary said nothing. She could see the hunger in Eanna's eyes, and the dread of losing a lottery. She slowly turned her head and looked at Sarah who sat on the dirt floor leaning against the wall of the dugout with her eyes closed. She would wake soon and need to feed. Mary winced. She could not deny it. Eanna was right. They needed to leave the pit and search for food.

"It will be light within two hours." Mary said. "We must make haste to return under cover of darkness. Sarah will stay here with Althea."

"Yes, Priestess, as you wish." Her eyes now gleamed. She turned to inform the others and excitement grew within the pit.

Mary woke Sarah and instructed her to stay with Althea. She would go with them, but would watch from afar so as to escape should the others be seen by an early rising villager. She could not risk there being no one to protect the offspring.

Mary was the last to leave the pit. Her coven was standing in the small room of the stone shelter waiting for her to join them. Their eyes were wide and unblinking as they looked from one to the other. They stood frozen in time, afraid to leave the safety of the shelter, yet more afraid of what fate awaited them if they didn't. Mary moved closer to the door and listened. She could hear only a gentle breeze shaking the leaves of the quaking aspens that loomed above them.

"Go forth two by two, and stay away from the village. If you are seen and followed, thou shalt not return to the shelter. You will be on your own hence forth. Do you understand?" Mary's stern words brought a sobering realization to them all.

"Yes, Priestess," they answered as they nodded their heads.

Mary slowly opened the door and sniffed the night air. It smelled of wet grass from a recent evening shower coupled with the pungent saltiness from the ocean. She stepped out into the darkness and quietly walked about ten feet straight out from the doorway. She barely took a breath as she listened to the sounds of the night. Once she knew they were alone, she motioned for the others to join her. Placing a boney finger to her lips, she warned the others not to speak. Once they were beside her she gave her final instruction.

"Be wise when making a kill. Allow not the animal to make a sound. Wrap it tightly in pieces of your clothing that it not drip blood and leave a trail. Now go, and be back before the eastern sky lightens."

Without a word they headed off into the woods, keeping low yet moving swiftly. They split up to hunt in groups of two as instructed. Eanna, being the most experienced of the group chose the poorest tracker to go with her. Eanna surmised she was the youngest of the coven members and would most likely not question her direction. It made her feel superior and triumphant to display her role of authority. She led her protégée further away from the others, in through the dense pines and out into a clearing. She waved her hand down toward the ground as she crouched and the girl mimicked Eanna's movements.

"Stay still, Rachel," Eanna whispered, "and don't make a sound. I must go alone from here, lest we attract attention."

"Attention? Eanna, are we close to the village? The Priestess warned us not to go there."

"Hush, child!" Eanna spun around and locked eyes with the girl. Quickly she placed her hand over Rachael's mouth. "Question not my judgment. Do you think the Priestess really cares if we find food or not? She would just as soon feed us to the offspring. Tell me, which leg do you wish to be taken?" Eanna grabbed the girl's thighs, one with each hand, and squeezed them hard.

The girl drew in a sharp breath, then her lips thinned as her mouth tightened firmly against her yellowed teeth. "I shall not be a part of this!" Spit spewed through her teeth and sprayed Eanna's face. There was fear in her eyes, but she held her ground against Eanna.

"As I said," Eanna spoke firmly, "stay still and don't make a sound." Eanna stared at Rachael for what seemed an eternity, and looked away only when she felt she once again had the upper hand.

Eanna slowly pushed off the ground and peered

over the tall field grass. In the distance she could see a stone wall divider running across the center of the field and knew beyond it was a farmer's property. She could hear her own heart thudding and feel the throb of her pulse against her ear drums and in the sides of her neck. She could only hope that the Priestess was preoccupied with watching the others, because if she was to find them near the villagers her wrath would be inconceivable.

She moved slowly across the field staying low to the ground, pausing from time to time and listening carefully for any sounds of life. Then suddenly she heard a bleat in the distance. Her mouth immediately watered. She rose up and turned her head from side to side, trying desperately to decipher from which direction the sound came from. Finally a second bleat. A smile curled the edges of her lips and her eyes narrowed as they peered through the trees at the edge of the field. Just beyond the trees was another clearing and Eanna could plainly see the backside of a shed. Excitement fluttered in her belly and she could hardly stop herself from running at full speed toward the building, but she restrained her enthusiasm and tried to proceed with caution.

She crept upon the shed hiding within its shadow that was cast in the moonlight. She strained to hear. It was at first quiet, then she heard clucking. Chickens were not what she was risking her life for. She wanted red meat. She ventured out from behind the shed and could now see the barn and the owner's dwelling. The house was dark. She let herself draw a breath and then crept to the barn and leaned against the side of the building. Hearing no signs of life from the house, she slithered around the corner and went to the barn door. Slowly she lifted the latch and went inside. The sweet smell of hay that filled the air, mingled with the raunchy odor of dung.

Eanna looked around for her first victim.

A goat got to its feet and looked at her through the wooden slats of a stall. Eanna stared back and swallowed the saliva that had pooled in her mouth. She would have to make the kill quickly to prevent the animal from making noise. Her eyes searched the dark walls of the barn and finally found a scythe. She grabbed the scythe's long handle and pulled it from the wall. On the way back to the stall she spotted a bucket with some feed in it and at once she had an idea. She scooped it up and poured some of the feed out on the floor in front of the goat. When it lowered its head to eat, Eanna placed the curved blade of the scythe under the goat's throat and with all her strength she pulled up quickly on the blade pulling it toward her and slit the goat's throat. The goat went down with a thud into a growing pool of blood.

Eanna opened the gate to the stall and bent down to drink of the salty, life's blood of the goat. It was warm and took the edge off her hunger. Time stood still while she feasted, licking and tearing at the flesh with her teeth. Then she heard a noise that nearly stopped her heart from beating. Her head tilted back to face the darkness with her mouth agape and blood dripping off her teeth, and she listened to the racket coming from the chicken shed. There was scuffling and chickens clucking and fluttering around against the walls of the shed. Then came a noise that was from Eanna's worst nightmare, the sound of the door of the house being flung open and the footsteps of the farmer running down the porch steps. She heard him sliding a lead ball into the barrel of his musket and shoving the ramrod into the barrel as he packed the powder in tightly. Eanna watched through a crack of the door as the farmer went around the barn toward the shed.

"You low down varmint, get away from my chickens." The man yelled as he wrestled with the latch on the door. "I'm gonna make a stole for my wife outa you!" He yanked the door open and it hit the front side of the shed with a loud whack. He stopped in his tracks and looked into the coop. "What the ---Hey! Who are you? And what in tarnation are you doing with my chickens?"

Just as he started to take a step forward, Eanna stepped on a stick directly behind him and it made a loud crack as it snapped in two. He whipped around to see her just as she thrust the tip of the scythe through his torso. His mouth fell open and blood ran out of it and dripped off his chin. As he dropped to his knees and fell forward lying face down on the ground, Eanna looked straight ahead into the shed and into the eyes of Rachael. She was in a crouched position holding a dead chicken in her teeth. Feathers and blood were everywhere and there were at least two more chickens laying on the floor with their heads bitten off.

"What have you done?" Eanna asked her. The girl only shook her head with the chicken still held tightly in her teeth.

"Harold?" A woman's voice came from the house. "Harold, you answer me or I'll have to come out there."

Eanna and Rachael froze in their positions. They stared at one another until they heard the house door open, and then Rachael opened her mouth and let the chicken drop to the floor of the shed. Both of them knew what needed to be done now. There was no other choice. Eanna turned and walked to the house.

The attack was swift and without mercy or compassion. It was cold and ruthless, and it made Eanna feel incredible. This night *she* made the decisions. *She* took on the responsibility. And *she* would reap the rewards.

"Check the dwelling. No one lives." She ordered Rachael into the house, and Rachael dared not disobey.

They found two young ones in their beds and ended their lives viciously. The small farmhouse walls were speckled red and the floors were covered with bloody footprints. Eanna grabbed one blood soaked body and dragged it around on the floor to erase all of their footprints. Then they walked out of the farmhouse calmly, dragging a blanket behind them until they stepped off the porch onto the ground.

Eanna walked to the barn and pulled out the goat. She let it drop with a thud at Rachael's feet. She looked Rachael square in the face. "We found this goat wandering in the woods. It put up a fight, but we won. Is that understood?" She glared at Rachael.

"Yes." She nodded her head several times.

"Good. Now take off your robe and wrap the wound well. We don't want to leave a trail."

With desperate haste she tore her robe off herself and began wrapping the wound on the goat's neck. Once secure, Eanna bent down and ripped off the hem of her robe and tied it around the goat's front legs. She tore off another piece and tossed it to Rachael, and she tied the hind legs together as Eanna had done. Then Eanna slipped her hand under the knot and picked up the front legs of the goat and Rachael followed suit and picked up the hind legs and they walked back through the woods towards the shelter.

The closer they got to the shelter the more

nervous Eanna became. She knew the Priestess could see into their thoughts. For all she knew, Mary may have even watched the attack at the farm. She had the power to do so. Returning to the shelter could be a death sentence, but Eanna knew without the coven she would surely die anyway. Suddenly she heard voices just beyond the trees and knew in the next few minutes her questions would be answered.

"Hark, I think I hear them coming." One of them said.

"So do I," said another. "Wait until they see what we got."

Eanna turned and looked at Rachael just before she stepped out of the woods. Rachael looked back at her and said nothing, but Eanna could see in her eyes that she was committed to do as she was told to do. With that, Eanna pushed forward through the brush and out into the open area in front of the shelter.

The smiles and laughter stopped as soon as the others saw them holding the goat. They all looked down at the two dead opossums on the ground in front of the door, then at the goat. The smiles drained off their faces, but in their eyes Eanna could see the eagerness to satisfy their hunger.

"We have been awaiting your return. It is nearly dawn." One of the women said. "It was crossing our minds that perhaps you had been seen and could not return to us."

"No, that has not been the case. Our prey had, without a doubt, put up a more vigorous fight than your little opossums." Eanna belittled their kill. "Has no one else returned with any game?"

"No. The others have already returned to the pit." The women bent down, picked up the two opossums and went into the shelter.

Eanna turned to look at Rachael and her eyes silently told the girl to remember her instructions, and a brief nod in return put Eanna's mind at ease. Feeling in control, she turned around to enter the shelter and came face to face with Mary. Eanna gasped and nearly dropped her end of the goat.

"Priestess, you startled me." Eanna forced a laugh. "I did not see you."

"But I saw you." Mary said sternly.

Eanna could feel her looking straight through her and her only thought was that she hoped her death would be fast coming and without torture.

"Rachael, you may join the others inside, I will help Eanna with the goat," she said.

"As you wish, Priestess." Rachael quickly dropped her end of the goat and went inside.

"Seems I have underestimated you, Eanna. You are quite the hunter, aren't you?"

"We merely had better luck than the others. That is all."

"Is that so? Tell me, how is it that the others scoured these woods and could find only two measly opossums and you find a fat goat?"

"A wild goat, Priestess."

"A fat goat, Eanna."

Mary studied her for some time, so long it made her feel like running, but instead she showed her respect and lowered her eyes, bowing slightly. "Yes, Priestess."

"I trust you have left no trail?"

"No, Priestess. No trail."

"Mark my words, what you have done this night will not be without consequence, Eanna."

"Forgive me, but this I have done … for Sarah."

There was a long pause, then Mary said, "Come then, the others await us and they are hungry."

Eanna followed Mary back into the shelter, dragging the dead animal behind her.

The horde feasted for many days before having to venture out again for food. When they did, they stayed close to the shelter, only finding small critters like chipmunks and squirrels, and each time they returned with less and less. It was now late fall and winter would soon be upon them. Mary sat in the center of the pit and closed her eyes. Her mind took flight and she traveled over the area around them. Through the woods and fields and then came upon a farm. She found it to be overrun with villagers. Some mourning the dead and others declaring vengeance against the murderers or beasts that were responsible for the massacre. She watched the small army fan out from the farm with various weapons clutched in their hands.

Suddenly, Mary's eyes flashed open and she looked directly at Eanna. "Did I not say thine actions would not be without consequence? We cannot leave this place again. They hunt for the murderer."

Eanna's face went pale and she sat down and leaned against the wall of the pit. She knew there would be no lottery this time. When the coven could no longer control their hunger, she would be the chosen one. Day or night passed, they could not tell which from within the pit. All they knew was that they were growing hungrier with each passing moment.

"Mary", the feeble voice of Althea called out to the darkness of the pit.

Mary was startled. It was the first time that Althea had called her by her first name. She quickly crossed the dugout room and knelt at Althea's side. Althea reached out a feeble hand and grasped the front of Mary's robe. She pulled her down to speak in her ear. Her voice was weak, yet demanding.

"Let not my death be in vain," she whispered.

Mary tore herself away from Althea's grip and looked at her with both anger and dismay. "Ye know not what ye ask of me. I cannot allow it."

"Please," Althea begged. "Grant me this."

"Thou has always been with me, Althea, and thou always shall be."

"I cannot, my daughter. Thou must allow the ritual."

"No!" Mary shouted, but her refusal was not directed at Althea. The denial was for the persistent voice within her own heart that shouted, *"Yes! Yes!"*

"She is right, Priestess," Eanna spoke up. She squatted on the ground behind Mary. "Althea has served the coven well, and the time has come for her to pass on her gifts."

Mary spun around and faced Eanna with such anger that Eanna recoiled from the rage she saw in Mary's eyes. She fell backward, landing hard on her backside. Mary hacked and spewed spit through her few remaining teeth and it struck Eanna squarely in the face. She dared not to wipe if off and the spittle dripped off her chin and ran down her neck.

Mary then turned back to Althea and looked into the eyes she had known since she was a babe. For a moment she felt love for Althea. A feeling Mary hadn't experienced in many years. She saw in the old woman's eyes, pain and sadness, and yes, even fear. But most of all, she could see her dying mother's last request, and it both saddened and elated her. Mary knew Althea could see her struggle and would not allow her to be weak. Weakness was sure to bring the wrath of the Master upon them all, and she knew what torment eternity would deliver if the offspring did not live.

"If not for me, my daughter, then for Sarah," Althea pleaded.

Mary dropped her eyes, for she could refuse nothing for Sarah. Quickly, she turned away from Althea and wiped away the slick drool that had run to the corner of her mouth. She could deny herself no longer; she, too, hungered for the power that could sustain life.

The room was dead silent. Mary's eyes flashed open, and the hearts of the coven leaped in their chests. With the power of sheer will, a narrow table that rested against the earthen wall of the pit, slid across the dirt floor, and stopped in the center of the room. Mary walked to the table. She held out her hands and a black candle appeared in each of them. She placed one on each end of the table, then waved her hands over them and they blazed to life with a blue flame that cast a strange hue within the pit.

"Bring the elder," Mary ordered.

Eanna scrambled to her feet with the help of two coven members, and they picked up Althea and carried her to the table. They placed her face down on the bench and removed her robe. Her bare back now served as an altar. She said nothing.

Mary outstretched her arms, her fingertips nearly touching the blue flames of the black candles. "Let us pray," she said, and the coven recited the Lord's Prayer–in reverse.

Mary then lifted an inverted cross above her head and spoke the language of the Master. There was a flash of excitement in her eyes and a short gasp for air, then she thrust the crucifix into the center of Althea's back, penetrating the walls of her, still beating, heart. The crucifix became as a fountain, spewing the river of life. Mary filled a cup and drank from it, then passed it to Sarah.

"Drink, my daughter. For as oft as ye drink–so shall ye live."

Sarah placed the cup to her lips and tilted the bottom up, feverishly swallowing the warm blood. She lowered the vessel only after the last drop had flowed into her mouth. "More," she said with painted lips, then lowered her head to the lick at the red pool on the bench.

Althea, with the last of her strength, lifted her face from the table. Her eyes were glossed over with pain. "Hoc est corpus meum ..." she spoke, saying, "Take eat: this is my body, which was broken for you..."

Mary was the first to partake of the elder's power. She pulled the cross from Althea's back, reached into the wound, and removed her heart. It beat three times while clutched in her hand, then she did eat.

Sarah was next, as she gorged herself on the gushing organ. The others then came to the table in a flurry, devouring Althea's remains so as to inherit her power and extend their lives. The coven feasted for hours until their life-force was satisfied.

Eanna pushed up from the table and her eyes locked with Mary's. For a moment she looked as if she was going to run as she backed away, but instead, bowed her head and stared down at the bloody crucifix at her feet.

"Art thou ready to assume the honor of the eldest?" Mary asked her.

"Yes, Priestess, I am ready." Her voice wavered.

Mary pointed down at the bloody crucifix that lay on the floor. "Then take up thy cross and follow me." She turned and walked away from the table where the bony carcass of Althea lay.

Eanna picked up the crucifix and eagerly followed Mary to the far corner of the dugout room. She stood facing Mary's back, beaming with the excitement of being crowned elder.

"Art thou prepared to meet thy destiny?" Mary asked. She stood with her face nearly touching the dirt wall.

"I am," Eanna answered.

"Then behold, thy chosen path," Mary said as she turned swiftly and slashed the front of Eanna's torso with her sharp talons. Her intestines spilled out onto the dirt floor, and while she stood in shock of her demise, waiting for death to come, she watched the faithful feast upon her innards.

***

And so the years passed, and the Inheritance Ritual was repeated nine times over, until the only two to remain living were Mary and Sarah Deven. Each time they feasted they grew more powerful, and their lives were renewed. Sarah had aged little, but Mary–being the sole provider of sustenance for Sarah–withered, her bones twisted with a debilitating disease. But death would not come to her. Not yet. They wandered out into the night, searching for souls to quench their thirst, and returned each night to the safety of the dugout before light streaked the eastern sky.

Many years passed and Mary had begun to fear the Master had forsaken her. It was becoming harder to find enough food and she had resorted to stealing from the villager's stables. On one occasion, the painful bleat of a goat had awakened its owner, and Mary had to leave the animal to drown in its own blood in order to escape being discovered. She wanted to go back and kill the owner as well and was angry that she had to restrain herself from doing so. But she did. For Sarah. As she returned to the stone shelter that night, Sarah was waiting outside to be fed, and Mary, again, gave herself to the offspring, wincing with pain as Sarah struggled to quench her hunger.

Mary looked up to the black heavens and cried out, "Why has thou forsaken me?"

A loud clap of thunder tore the heavens and from a dark cloud the Master appeared. Mary fell to the ground with respect for him, while Sarah stood, wide-eyed, admiring her father.

"Mary, Mary," he said softly, "have I not given to you life everlasting?"

"Yes, Master."

"Hast thou lost faith in me?"

"No, Master."

"Then take Sarah and go down into the pit and wait until I call you out, for the time is not yet." He then removed from under his sash his Black Book and placed it in Mary's hands. "Remember, Mary," he said as his eyes sparkled, "to keep it … holy."

She nodded her solemn promise, and the Beast disappeared. Wasting no time, she led Sarah down into the pit, and the door was sealed up. There, in the dark, earthy cellar they waited for the sound of their Master's voice to call them forth—and they were hungry.

And it shall come to pass in the last days, saith God, I will pour out my spirit upon all flesh: and your sons and your daughters shall prophesy, and your young men shall see visions, and your old men shall dream dreams:

Acts 2:17

CHAPTER 3–THE DREAM

Peter Amado squirmed in the seat behind the wheel of his '99 Sunbird for the zillionth time since he had left the Salton Sea. The desert sand had found its way into the car's bucket seat and now felt like sand paper against the backs of his sunburned thighs. Though the peaks of the Santa Rosa Mountains beckoned him on toward San Diego, he knew he would soon have to pull off the road and stretch his legs, for they had already gone stiff with the swelling that accompanied the sunburn.

He wasn't in all that big of a rush to get there anyway. He was being sent "again" to investigate another so-called haunting. The job was with a group assigned to do 30 minute segments for one of the more successful television weeklies. The pay was good, but at times the false leads reminded him of the days he'd worked as a Paranormal Investigator for a well-known debunking organization in Buffalo, New York. He had seen more kooks than he cared to count and it seemed everyone had a ghost story to tell. Even though as many as ninety-eight percent of all reports of haunting phenomenon have natural explanations, Peter knew it to not always be the case, for he had witnessed it firsthand. On each of these occasions he presented the organization with the truth and they discarded his evidence. It just didn't fit into their realm of ideas.

So Peter quit the organization and struck out on his own, until hooking up with the stars of fright night TV. He knew the real thing to be out there, and he'd investigate every haunting, poltergeist, medium, and psychic to prove it. A flutter spread its wings in his stomach. Perhaps this haunting would turn out to be authentic. Maybe he'd even get something on video tape. Wouldn't he love to cram that up their high held Buffalo noses.

Deke Crandell, the director of the prime time hit paranormal show, was totally convinced that something extraordinary was at work at a house on Flintridge Drive in Paradise Hills. And that said a lot for Deke. He was the crew's number one skeptic. He had begged Peter to come to San Diego, promising a substantial bonus if it panned out. Peter had never known Deke to be so free with his allotted budget. That alone was enough to persuade Peter to make the trip. Then, of course, there was the quiver in Deke's voice. Peter had heard that nervous stutter once before in his life, and knew right then and there he had to make the trip to the west coast.

The sensation of pins and needles in his legs forced him to concentrate on the present. Just as he was about to pull off on the side of the road the Sunbird's headlights illuminated a sign that said, "Lookout Point." He slowed the car and pulled into the turnout lane stopping beside a huge rock. In the boulder a metal plate had been embedded with cement, no doubt, describing the area below to any tourist that might be interested. He got out of the car and stood for a moment, trying to get used to the pressure in his swollen legs, then shuffled to the rear of the car and opened the trunk.

Inside was his every possession. He had lived in his car for the past month, and this lifestyle was getting old. He longed for something other than campground showers and the cramped backseat of the Sunbird. Deke had promised him a hotel room when he reached San Diego, and he was definitely going to take him up on the offer. He rummaged around in the trunk and finally found a pair of sweat pants and pulled them on over his shorts. He winced with pain, and shuttered to think of how burned he would have been had it not been for the change in the wind direction. He had fallen asleep earlier that day on the bank of the Salton Sea with a gentle breeze blowing off the desert, and was awakened once the wind began blowing from across the water. Years of chemical runoff and dehydration had polluted the water. Bacteria and disease was rampant. Many fish had succumbed to the oxygen deprived water and the smell of decaying fish was more than his nasal passages could tolerate. Thankfully he was far from the stench now, and he drew in a deep breath of the cool, night air.

He scuffed around the car with his worn leather sandals slapping his heels and tried to walk off the stiffness. He went to the edge of the overlook and peered down. All he could see was darkness. It didn't matter. He knew what was below—more desert. He also knew, had he been able to see, that in all likelihood, the most exciting view would have been the metal plate in the rock describing what had happened there so many years ago. But, without a flashlight, that too, wore a black shroud.

As the tightness in his legs subsided he went back to the car, opened the door, and eased himself into the driver's seat, but he couldn't bring himself to turn the ignition key. He sat there staring out into the darkness, listening to the crickets' lullaby. A heaviness replaced the pain of his sunburn and with its relief came sleep. It washed over him so quickly he was unable to resist it, and his subconscious was catapulted into a familiar dreamscape.

He was standing in a gray, desolate place. A place without form, and void, where sadness and despair were born. In a place that was the pit of all evil he cried out for mercy, to be freed from the torment that he had come to know as Hell. But no relief came. Through the haze of his tears he could see images forming in the darkness. Faceless forms, as black as sin, circled him. They poked, prodded, and scratched him with hands he couldn't see. Then he felt excruciating pain as sharp teeth bit down on his shoulder!

He woke with a jolt! Recklessly, he foraged for the car door handle, somewhere between reality and the realm of sleep, trying desperately to escape the confines of his dream. Just as there seemed to be no escape, his hand grasped the latch and the door swung open and dumped him out onto the pavement, leaving him full of anxiety. His breath came out of him in short rapid exhales and he tried to gain control of his breathing and slow his heartbeat.

What did the dream mean? It was coming to him more often and each time he was remembering more of it. He sat there on the pavement, leaning against the cold metal of his car and tried to recall the images before they faded from his memory. It was no use, the forms in his dream were shrouded in darkness and they soon faded like a blackbird flying into the night.

The dry night air drifting over the Painted Desert no longer smelled of sweet cactus blooms, but of a musty odor that pervaded the area, and filled Peter's mouth with the taste of bitter soil. He pulled himself up and leaned against the side of his car. The top of his left shoulder blade began to sting and he reached back with his right hand and touched it. His fingertips felt the stickiness of moist blood seeping through his shirt and again his heart began to thud. A voice that he recognized to be his own, screamed inside his mind, pleading with his logical intelligence to not pursue the discovery any further. To leave the injury alone. To make himself believe the wound was the result of his fall from the car. Nothing else. But it was as if his physical being was totally detached from what he was thinking, and defiant, refusing to listen to the demands of his wishful thinking. And with that, his hand reached beneath his shirt and felt the horror that he so desired to never know. The wounds were deep and jagged, and shaped like the devilish grin that had sunk its teeth deeply into his flesh in his latest of nightmares. He felt the blood ooze from the deepest of the wounds, wetting through the fabric of his shirt, and quickly, consciously, he withdrew his hand. Vomit came up in his throat and he broke out in a cold sweat. He swallowed hard, and his throat burned as he forced the acid of his stomach back down. *How could this be?* His mouth salivated and he spit again and again as he tried to get rid of the lingering taste of dirt that filled his mouth.

An unease had set in–as always after the dream–and he no longer wanted to be alone in the darkness. He longed for the city lights and the laughter of people that would tell him he was crazy to let a dream upset him like this. But he wasn't crazy. He only wished he was. At least then there would be a reasonable explanation for the fear he was experiencing. Maybe he imagined the teeth marks, too. He had heard of dreams carrying over into wakefulness. Perhaps he was still dreaming when he felt the teeth marks on his shoulder. He knew of only one way to be certain, but he wasn't going to look again to be sure. Not yet.

Was he being watched? He whipped around and searched the road, certain he was not alone, but he saw no one. Only the stillness of the night stared back at him. He let out a long sigh, then shook his head as he let out a faint laugh. Surely he was losing his mind. He shuddered when he realized how desperately he welcomed insanity as opposed to what he feared to be the truth.

With both hands he reached behind him and grasped the car door latch and pulled up on it, stepping forward just enough to allow the door to be opened. He turned to the right slightly and stepped sideways and squeezed through an opening that was just wide enough to let him slip into the seat. He then closed the door behind him in an attempt to insure nothing else got in with him. The keys jingled as he nervously turned the ignition switch and the engine roared to life. Again he shook his head in shame that he was letting his imagination run wild. So be it, he thought, as he sped away and refused to look back, and he didn't stop until he reached the hotel in the El Cajon valley.

It was 10 pm when Peter walked through the lobby doors of the hotel with his garment bag hung over his right shoulder. He could barely see the top of the clerk's head behind the computer screen that sat on the desk. As Peter stepped up to the counter, he got a better look at the man. He was quite overweight, with straight, dark brown hair that appeared oily and fell forward over his forehead and hung over his left eye. A couple strands moved slightly every time he blinked. He was dressed in a long sleeved, white shirt that hadn't seen an iron in only God knows when, and its tail was tucked into a pair of black pants. He wore a black belt that disappeared between rolls of fat once it passed midway around his front torso. He seemed mesmerized by what was on his computer screen, with one hand on his mouse and the other holding a half-eaten, powdered sugar donut.

Peter cleared his throat in an attempt to catch the young man's attention. He glanced at Peter briefly then began clicking his left mouse button. Peter surmised he was closing windows on his screen trying to hide what he had been viewing. There was a final click and then he turned to Peter, blinking his eyes several times as if trying to regain his focus on the real world.

"May I help you, sir?" he asked with a donut crumb still stuck in the corner of his mouth. Peter dropped his eyes and looked away for a second, not wanting to stare. The man must have sensed his unease and swiped at his powdered sugared lips. "Ah, sorry, I didn't have a thing to eat all day and I was starving." He wiped his hand off on the side of his pant leg. "Care for a donut?" he asked, lifting the box and opening the lid.

"No, thank you. Just a room please."

"Do you have a reservation?"

"I believe so. I'm Peter Amado. My employer made

the reservation."

The clerk looked back to his computer screen and began typing. "Yeah, I've gotcha right here, Mr. Amado. We've got your room all set for you." He passed Peter a room key. "Will you be needing more than one pass key?"

"No. Just the one will do nicely."

"Alrighty then. Room 212." He swiveled his chair around and removed an envelope that had been tacked to a bulletin board behind him and slid it up on the counter in front of Peter. "The gentleman that reserved the room for you asked me to give this to you the second you arrived."

"Thanks." Peter placed his hand over the envelope and slid it towards himself and slipped it in his pocket. The clerk's eyes looked a little disappointed that Peter didn't open it right away. Being a hotel desk clerk must be quite a dull life, Peter thought, and wondered if he'd like to change places. He chuckled to himself as he turned and walked to the elevator.

"Wake up call, sir?"

"8 am."

"Yes, sir." The clerk raised his voice as the doors were closing on the elevator. "Hey, the room's on the 2nd floor and to your right. If you ..." The door closed in mid-sentence.

Yeah, it's a dull life, Peter concluded as the elevator ascended. Before the door opened on the second floor, Peter had opened the note from Deke. He urged Peter to come as soon as possible and included a map to the house on Flintridge Drive. Deke's persistence was really starting to make Peter curious, but it would have to wait. Sleep was going to take top billing for what remained of the night. He unlocked his room, threw down his garment bag on a chair, and walked straight to the bed and collapsed, face down, with Deke's note still clutched in his hand.

Several hours of uninterrupted sleep seemed to be over in an instant, and Peter struggled to pull himself from the bed. He sat on the edge, still groggy with sleep, and felt a twinge as his left shoulder began to sting. He reached up and touched it and felt several little scabs. In an instant he was wide awake! The night before flashed before him. It hadn't been a dream. *Something* had bitten him. Not wanting to believe it, he yanked his hand away and tried to push it from his mind. He couldn't think about that now; he had to get to the house on Flintridge Drive. He got up, showered and shaved—being careful not to even look at his shoulder. He dressed, complete with suit coat and tie, and soon he was out the door and on his way.

Deke had given him excellent directions and within twenty minutes he was pulling over to the curb parallel to the house on Flintridge. He sat there a minute and looked around, thinking of how the house looked like every other dwelling in San Diego County. It was, after all, your typical light tan stucco, with a small fenced yard. He got out of his car and walked around to the front of the house. It was hard to believe that anything supernatural could be at work in such a civilized community, but it was. He could feel it as he approached the small, single family dwelling. He opened the gate of the chain-link fence and crossed the boundary into the presence of something evil. The air didn't move inside the fenced yard, and Peter felt as if a weight was pressing down on the top of his head.

He could see the crew inside the house setting up camera equipment and taking readings from various sensors. Deke was standing just inside the screen door. He was a short, chubby man, and Peter had never seen him without beads of sweat on his forehead. Today he seemed to be sweating more than most. He was a redhead with very pale skin, but this morning his color looked a little gray. He glanced up and saw Peter and it was obvious he couldn't wait to talk to him. He threw open the screen door and hustled down the steps to meet him, with spit spraying from his mouth as he talked. Peter had never seen him so excited.

"My God, Peter, it's incredible! We've got readings off the scale. Electromagnetic abnormalcies, abnormal radiation levels, unusual levels of other gases, you name it, Peter, we've got it! It's every freakin' thing we've been wishing for." Deke lifted a long arm exposing a yellowed, circular perspiration stain in the armpit of his wrinkled shirt and squeezed Peter around the shoulders as they walked up the steps to the screen door that had just finished closing after Deke's dramatic exit. Peter winced.

"Oh, sorry." Deke realized Peter's discomfort. "Sunburn?"

"Something like that," Peter answered, remembering the teeth marks on his shoulder. Suddenly he had a chill.

"I thought you Italian boys didn't burn." Deke laughed and patted him on the shoulder. Peter wasn't amused, and Deke quickly removed his hand.

"What can you tell me about the people that live here?" Peter wanted to get down to business. Finding the real thing hadn't excited him as it had Deke. There was a part of him, somewhere deep in his gut, that wouldn't allow him to feel joy at witnessing something so evil.

"Just one guy lives here. His name is Roberto Sanchez. And Peter, he's really out of it. He just sits there on the sofa, staring off into space. Maybe you can get through to him. We've been trying since last night." Deke shook his head.

"Has anyone tried to get him professional help?"

"Oh yeah, he's been in a doctor's care for about six months. That's his sister over there," he said as he pointed to a small dining area just inside to the left. "Her name is Maria Rosario. She says the doctor just keeps him doped up."

"Well, that sure doesn't do much for the credibility of his story," Peter whispered.

"Screw him," Deke smiled, "with what we've got, we don't need him." He patted Peter on the back and noticing Peter's wince, quickly lifted his hand, saying sorry, then he opened the door and stepped aside to let Peter go in first. "Trust me. You'll see." His eyes had a knowing twinkle in them.

Peter stepped over the threshold and was struck by an unseen force that knocked the air out of him and made him place his arms across his middle for protection should there be another blow.

"A real kick in the gut, huh, Pete?" Deke teased. His eyes reminded Peter of The Hobbit.

"Thanks for the warning, pal. I owe you one," he wheezed.

"Not to worry, buddy, the pain subsides the longer you're here. Since yesterday afternoon it has diminished to what we all agree is mild nausea."

"Is that your way of telling me I have something to look forward to?" Peter massaged the hardness in his belly and the pain subsided enough that he could finally draw a decent breath.

Peter stood with his back to the door getting familiar with his surroundings. The room was filled with smoke and crowded with people, each one going about their assigned duties. A group had gathered around the dining room table, which was loaded down with every type of electronic equipment money could buy. Computers, VCRs, monitors, tape recorders, and meters for taking levels of radiation, temperature, and various gases. There was a steady stream of people going in and coming out of a back bedroom, some having to turn sideways in the hallway to pass each other, and a constant murmur of conversation filled the house.

A man, about the age of sixty, sat round shouldered on the far end of a frayed, blue flowered sofa, unaffected by the circus of enthusiasts. A floor lamp stood in the corner of the room, and ignored by the light of day, remained lit, casting a yellow tint to the man's face. He held a glass ash tray on his lap and it was filled with cigarette butts standing upright in the ashes. Between his nicotine stained fingers he held a Camel cigarette that had burned up to the filter. Its long gray ash had curled under, and was threatening to fall over his lap. Not that he would have noticed, or cared.

Peter had seen the look before. It was a vacant, fixed gaze. He knew the man was visiting a place far away. A place in the darkness, where evil dwells.

He felt compelled to speak to the old man, but Deke grabbed his arm and pulled him toward the dining room table. Deke tapped one of the sound crew members on the shoulder and removed the head phones from the guy's head.

"Give this a listen, Pete," he gloated. He passed the head phones to Peter, who then placed the bulky phones over his ears and listened. "Can you hear it?" Deke was anxious.

Peter shook his head back and forth, and Deke motioned to the sound man to up the volume. A blast of sound bombarded Peter's eardrums and he yanked the headphones away from his ears.

"Wow! Wouldn't you say, Peter?" Deke giggled. "It sounds like squealing pigs to me. God awful, isn't it? And it's coming from inside the walls of this house."

The sounds made Peter sick. He had heard them before, in another place and time that he wished he could forget. It made no difference that he had placed years and miles between the incidents, evil had found him again.

"What do you make of it?" Deke asked.

"It's a sign."

"Of what?" Deke screwed up his face.

"Of a serious demonic infestation," he answered.

Everyone around the table stopped talking and looked up at Peter, including Maria Rosario, who quickly made the sign of the cross. She struggled to get around the others that stood around the table blocking her path, and stopped only when she stood face to face with Peter. She spoke to him in Spanish, and though he couldn't understand the language, he knew only too well what she was saying.

Deke waved his hand at her, trying to get a word

in. "You must forgive, Peter, Ms. Rosario, despite his dark hair and olive skin, he's Italian. You'll have to speak English."

"Si," she replied, then shook her head emitting a faint laugh. "I mean, yes, sir." She looked again at Peter. "Please, you can help my brother, yes?"

"I'll try, Maria," Peter said, "but first, I need you to tell me everything that has happened to Roberto."

"How can I explain what I don't understand?" She lowered her gaze and shook her head.

"Let me be the one to try and make sense of it all. Just tell me what happened here."

She looked across the room to where her brother sat slumped on the sofa. He looked about twenty years older than her, with deep scowl lines running across his forehead and a week's worth of gray stubble on his face and neck.

"It began about six months ago," she said, not once taking her eyes off her brother. "He called me one night about eleven o'clock. He said he had been attacked while in his bed by a scaly succubus, posing as a woman with a young body. As she straddled him in bed he said she transformed into an old woman as ugly as sin. He said she had blood red eyes and green gums." She shook her head with disbelief. "He said this 'thing' raped him." She covered her mouth with two shaky hands and tried to fight back the tears, but they spilled from her eyes and ran over the backs of her hands. "How can this be, Senior Peter?" She continued to cry.

Peter took her hands away from her face and held them in his own. "Tell me the rest."

"Well, he said while this happened he could see two figures. They were wearing black robes and were standing at the foot of his bed, chanting in a language he couldn't understand. I know this sounds loco, but he believes it happened. And you know what, Senior Peter?"

"What?"

"I believe him. I guess that makes me loco, too. Yes?" Her voice quivered and she looked afraid.

Peter squeezed her hands and reassured her that he wouldn't pass judgment. Her eyes met his, and he wouldn't release her gaze until he could see in her eyes that she believed and trusted him. Then he gently patted the back of her hand and smiled as he let go and turned his attention to her brother. He walked over to the sofa and sat down beside Roberto. A series of hushes could be heard throughout the house as everyone realized Peter's intentions of speaking with the old man. Peter could hear tape recorder buttons being pushed and was also aware of the camera man positioning himself opposite the sofa, and the hum of the zoom as it moved in and out. He never looked at any of them. He had something more important to do.

"Mr. Sanchez?" No answer. You could now hear a pin drop in the house. "Roberto, I have come to help you."

The old man closed his eyes and his head slowly turned to face Peter. The cameraman gasped and jerked his head away from the viewfinder as if to question what he was seeing through his lens. Others stood silent with their mouths hanging open, surprised by the old man's movement. Obviously, this was the most interaction they'd seen the old man engage in. Deke had his own way with dealing with what he didn't understand. He was using every expletive known to man. Peter raised a hand, demanding quiet and was relieved to be obeyed. Sanchez's mouth opened and a voice, low and raspy, cut through the silence in the room.

"You want to help me? You can't even help yourself–Peter." His voice was hoarse as he laughed, and it came from within the man, not his lips.

Peter knew the voice, and it didn't belong to Roberto Sanchez. "Who are you?" Peter demanded.

A laugh that belonged in an asylum for the insane came from Sanchez's throat, and his eyelids slowly opened to reveal a pair of glowing, yellow eyes. Peter tried to jerk away, but was held to the man's gaze. An unseen force grabbed him by the necktie and pulled him closer to the old man's face.

"You can't help this man," the demon spoke from within Sanchez. "He is with me."

"You can't have him," Peter said through clenched teeth. He felt his face go red with anger.

"But he is already mine," the demon replied. Its voice was low and throaty.

"No!" Peter grabbed a fistful of the man's shirt.

The corners of the old man's mouth slowly curled into a smile, and the yellow eyes glared solidly at Peter, telling him he would not, could not, win. The eyelids grew heavy and only after they were closed completely was Peter able to release the man's shirt and move away. He stood and backed into the center of the room, not once taking his eyes off the figure that was again just an old man, slumped on a sofa, showing no emotion.

"Deke," Peter beckoned, "clear the house."

"What?" Deke approached him, trying to be discreet, so as not to look like a fool in front of the whole crew. His voice became almost a whisper. "Are you nuts? We can't leave now. We'll all lose our jobs."

"Deke," Peter snarled through his teeth, "get everyone out of here–NOW!"

"Okay, okay. Jeez, take it easy, will ya." He waved, reluctantly, to the crew. "You heard him. Everybody out." They were all too happy to comply. Deke held out his arm, motioning the last two or three out the door, then he turned and started to follow them.

"Not you," Peter said to Deke.

"I *knew* you were going to say that. I just *knew* it."

"Show me the man's bedroom."

Deke shook his head and mumbled under his breath while he walked to the table and picked up a couple of meters and a temperature gauge. He grabbed a Geiger counter and shoved it into Peter's chest as he passed him. "Come on, then," he snarled, "let's get this over with." Deke always was better at giving the orders. He even looked awkward carrying the equipment as he walked ahead and led Peter into the old man's bedroom.

When Peter stepped through the bedroom doorway he didn't need a meter to gauge the level of static electricity. The hairs on his arms stood up. Deke walked to the foot of Sanchez's bed and waited for Peter to come further into the room. As he did, he studied the room's layout, getting a feel for the environment.

The bed was a twin size with a spring mattress that resembled a hammock because of the deep hollow it had down its middle. It was pushed up against the wall on the far side of the room, and beside it was a small night stand, littered with empty cans of Mountain Dew. A cowboy boot lamp with no shade and an overflowing ash tray also sat on the table. And flies. There must have been a thousand dead flies.

Peter was drawn to the bedside and was vaguely aware that Deke was talking to him. His voice seemed so far away that Peter could barely make out the words.

"Over here is where things really go wild," Deke said. He was holding a temperature gauge in his right hand and was waving it back and forth in front of him. "The temp drops fifteen degrees in this area. We've got video of a vaporous form over the bed," Deke mumbled, seeming more caught up in his gauges than what he was telling Peter, "but when we filmed this area we lost video."

Peter's head spun to face Deke. He was still studying his gauges. "What did you say?"

Deke looked at Peter. His eyes were full of haze. "What?"

"The video, Deke, what did you say about the video?"

"Oh, that. It was a blackout. We still don't know what caused it. Faulty equipment," he shrugged, "or what, but when the camera moved away from this area it began working again. Funniest thing."

"It wasn't the equipment," Peter replied.

"You know, before that old man in the living room spoke to you, I might have been able to argue that statement with you, but now, after that, after seeing his eyes like that, and that voice ...What was that anyway?

Have you ever seen such a thing? I mean to tell ya, it gave me the shivers," Deke rambled on. "Well I'm here to tell ya I hope to never see it again, Pete, it scared the crap out of me."

Peter tried to tell him that he had seen it once before, a long time ago, but the words wouldn't come. He shook his head. The demon was still at work on him, he was sure of it. It was trying to cloud his vision; to draw his attention away from the foot of the bed. The Geiger counter that he held at arm's length over the center of the bed clicked faster and louder the more he tried to concentrate on what Deke was saying. It took all of his willpower to open his hand and drop the sensor on the bed. He backed away and sidestepped closer to Deke.

Deke glanced up at Peter and looked a little concerned. "Hey, buddy, are you alright? You look a little pale. Maybe you should step outside for a while. After all, you haven't been inside the place for very long. You are probably still adjusting to the atmosphere in here. It took all of us nearly eight hours before we didn't feel like we were going to hurl our guts every fifteen minutes. Hey, you're not gonna blow lunch, are ya? You better step out before ..."

"No. There's something here for me to know. I feel it." Peter stood close to Deke with their elbows touching.

"Well, count me out of the psychic stuff, huh, buddy," Deke said as he stepped back. "You know that always gives me the heebie-jeebies."

Peter stepped forward, toward the foot of Sanchez's bed. He could hear Deke making tracks for the door, planting his feet down firmly on the floor. Then the footsteps came to an abrupt halt, and Peter could hear the fabric of his clothes swish as Deke turned to face him. A faint smile came to Peter's lips. Deke never could resist watching.

A tickle began in Peter's stomach. It was a familiar tug that told him he was about to have a vision. It was pulling him from the world of reality, and pushing him into the realm of darkness. He closed his eyes and let the unseen lead him where no other soul had trod.

He was in a dark place. A room? He wasn't sure. Black forms moved in the darkness. They circled him, chanting words that sounded garbled and far away. Each time the figures circled they came closer to him, until they were so close he could detect a scent on their clothing. The smell reminded him of his brother, Daniel, and a summer long ago when they had dug a huge hole in their backyard. They had hoped the rains would come and fill it up and give them a swimming hole for the summer. But the rains never came, and subsequently, he and his brother spent hours playing in the cool, damp hole, their clothes taking on the scent of a freshly dug grave. Peter was yanked back from the thoughts of his past and was aware the black forms had turned toward him. Nausea washed over him. He thought he was going to puke. The forms were taking shape and he was no longer in doubt. They were human forms. He couldn't see their faces. One moved in even closer than the others and he heard its voice clearly say, "Daniel is here."

Peter jumped back, and out of his vision. Deke was standing in front of him now, staring at him with huge, worried eyes. He didn't have an ounce of color in his face.

"That's it! We're outta here," he blurted. He ran his nervous fingers through his thinning, red hair. "I've been trying to get a response from you for over fifteen minutes! God Almighty, Peter, you know I can't take this sh ..."

Peter didn't hear the rest of what Deke had to say. He was already out through the front door of the house, vomiting beside the chain link fence. He could hear a low, raspy laugh coming from inside the house. Coming from Roberto Sanchez. Peter heaved again, then rested against a fence post. His clothes were scented with a pungent, musty odor and he couldn't get rid of the taste of dirt in his mouth.

Raging waves of the sea, foaming out their own shame; wandering stars, to whom is reserved the blackness of darkness forever.

Jude 13

CHAPTER 4–THE BOOK OF SHADOWS

Gregory Moore stood in one of the few remaining phone booths since the cell phone rage, just outside a small grill and gift shop on the waterfront of Salem, Massachusetts, a place called the Crystal Café. He was all but pacing inside the booth, shifting his weight from one foot to the other, while his left shoulder pressed the receiver to his ear. He wasn't usually the nervous type, but today was different. If he was right, in a few minutes he'd be meeting with someone, right here in The Crystal Café that could possibly change his whole life.

With a shaky palm he wiped the sweat from his forehead, slicking back his long, light blonde hair, as a droplet that hung over his upper lip spilled on his tongue and filled his mouth with its saltiness. New England was always known for its cool ocean breezes, but today was promising to be a scorcher. His dog, Phoenix, a stray German Shepard he had adopted while hitchhiking through Arizona, barked and pawed at the door. It was sweltering inside the booth, but Greg knew if he cracked the door an inch he'd be sharing the glass coffin with Phoenix, and it was just too hot to have that mutt breathing on him. So Greg held the door shut with his foot every time Phoenix jumped against it.

The phone began to ring on the other end of the line, and Greg braced himself for an old fashioned tongue lashing from his Miss-Goody-Two-Shoes twin sister. He wanted to hang up, to not have to explain his next get-rich-quick scheme to her, but he couldn't. She had always been there for him whenever he'd screwed up or had gotten in with the wrong crowd. The last time she bailed him out she made him promise to keep a good job and check in with her every Friday without fail. He hated to admit it, but it was working. He was becoming a regular working dude. For the past three weeks he had been working with a construction crew clearing a site for a new shopping center close to the historical sites and attractions of Salem. It was a mundane job–until three days ago. That was when he made perhaps the greatest occult find in history; a scroll that was sure to be worth a mint, and the envy of every occult antique dealer in the country. He knew she wouldn't understand, but he owed her the truth. So he was a dream chaser. He had never denied it. He knew she would laugh at him when he told her that this time was different. But it was. He could feel it.

Her answering machine switched on and he let out his breath, not realizing until that moment that he had been holding it. He wouldn't have to listen to her yelling at him after all, and that suited him just fine. By the time he was to call her again, he'd have the proof that this wasn't just another wild goose chase. He was going to prove to her, once and for all, that he could be a success at something. Something big.

The thought of it excited him and gave him a feeling of self-confidence, then the beep came signaling him to leave a message and he got sick to his stomach. He took a deep breath and said, "Hi, Sis! It's Greg. Just thought I'd let you know that I'm not working at the site anymore. Something has come up and I can't pass up the chance to follow through on it. I'll call you as soon as I know more. Love ya. Bye." He quickly hung up the phone and let out a deep breath, trying to push it from his mind. Right now, all he wanted to focus on was the person he was about to meet in The Crystal Café. The meeting had been set up by a woman named Miriam he'd met in an herb and vitamin shop near the construction site. She said that if anyone in Salem could translate the scroll, it would be this man.

Greg opened the door of the phone booth and stepped out of the sweat box. Phoenix yelped and jumped around him, no longer interested in getting into the booth. He led the dog around the side of the building and tied him to a drainpipe. Phoenix didn't like it much–he was a roamer much like Greg–but at least he would be in the shade. After a couple of scolding barks he laid down, and Greg walked casually around the front of the café and went inside.

The place was quiet and air-conditioned. A gift shop was to his right, displaying all shapes and sizes of crystal balls, wands, and the once so popular mood rings. To his left was a snack bar and about ten to twelve tables with chairs. A few couples sat here and there sipping coffee and talking quietly. Greg took a seat by the window and positioned himself so that he could see the door. Miriam hadn't given him a description of the man he was to meet, but–knowing the person's occupation–he thought someone dressed in all black was probably a good bet, as most witches that walked the streets of Salem wore black.

The minutes dragged on and no sign of his contact. The waitress brought him a second cup of coffee and he accepted it, though wished he'd asked for decaffeinated. He couldn't remember when he'd been so nervous. He dropped his eyes for a mere second and when he lifted them he was shocked to see a man standing right beside his table. The man was wearing a pair of jeans and a tan shirt. He had coal black hair and it was pulled back tightly in a ponytail.

"Mr. Moore," he said, offering to shake Greg's hand.

Greg slowly reached out and shook the man's hand, still unsure if this was the man he had been waiting for.

"We don't all wear black capes and carry a staff. We can look quite normal." He leaned in closer to Greg. "We can even look like you," he whispered. He didn't blink.

Greg swallowed hard. He wasn't sure he could trust the man. *What if word had gotten out about his find? His friend at the herb shop did like to talk. What if this guy was out for his own personal gain?*

"Relax, Mr. Moore," the man said as he sat down at the table, "I don't intend to steal your fame." He smiled showing his teeth. For a second Greg thought his canines looked to be extra-long, but then they returned to normal. Greg could feel his face go red. *Was he that obvious, or could this guy see things in him that no one else could?*

"I was told you need something translated."

Greg was relieved. "Yeah." His voice cut out as he spoke, reminding him of when he was a teenager, and he quickly cleared his throat to hide his nervousness. "Maybe I do. I guess that all depends on who I'm speaking to."

"Forgive me, I do seem to have the advantage. My name is Nigel Anguis. Miriam, the herbalist, sent me. Call her if you doubt me. I won't be offended."

"Not necessary, Mr. Anguis," Greg replied.

"Please, call me Nigel," he said. His voice was even and controlled.

"Nigel, I would hope you don't think me to be a fool. What I am about to show you is a copy. The original is in a safe place," Greg said with a smirk on his face. He thought for a second he saw disappointment in the man's eyes.

"Quite the contrary, Mr. Moore," the man replied. He, too, wore a grin.

Greg shifted in his seat and held his head high. He wasn't about to reciprocate by offering his first name. Being called Mister made him feel in control, and he wanted to keep it that way. He reached inside his shirt and pulled out the copy of the scroll, keeping his eyes locked to the man's gaze. Greg unfolded the three sheets of paper and placed them deliberately down in front of the man, but only after Greg dropped his eyes, did the man do the same. Greg suddenly had the feeling that the man was still staring at him, and he glanced up quickly to catch him in the act, but when he looked, the man was studying the scroll.

"What does it say?" Greg asked. His heart was pounding in his ears. *God, please let this be big.*

"Where did you get this?" he asked, refusing to lift his eyes from the inscriptions.

"Now, Nigel, we did agree that I'm not a fool. First tell me what it says."

"It's old alright. I'd say it dates back over three hundred years," he revealed.

"Three hundred? How do you know?" Greg's breath caught in his throat. *Yes, yes, this could be big!*

"Quite simple really," he answered bitterly. "It speaks of a ritual that hasn't been practiced–to my knowledge–since the senseless slaughter of my ancestors during the witch trials."

Greg couldn't hear the man's grief. He was too busy imagining how much money he could get for the scroll in the occult marketplace. The possibilities sent shivers down his spine.

"What does it say?" Greg pressed him.

"It speaks of a coven and a witch with considerable power. She was to be the holder of the Black Book."

"What Black Book?" Greg listened closely as the man's voice was no longer even and controlled.

"I'm sorry, you must forgive me, but this is astonishing. I had heard of such a coven, stories passed down through the generations, but no one was ever really sure of its existence."

"The book, Nigel, what about the book?" Greg was sitting on the edge of his seat. His sweaty palms pressed down on the small table and his fingers tapped nervously.

"Each coven has their own. It contains their laws, rituals, and the names of all who belong to the coven. It's as sacred to the coven as the Holy Bible is to Christians."

"Might I find it where I found the scroll?"

"Very doubtful. This scroll was written by a West Indian slave by the name of Ziea. It says the coven fled before the trials, and if it did, Mr. Moore, you can bet every cent you hope to gain from this, that the coven wouldn't have left without it."

"Does it say where they went?" Greg's fingertips danced on the table.

"No."

"You wouldn't be holding out on me, would you, Nigel?" Greg stared at him.

"I've told you all I know."

Greg tapped the bottom of the third page with a stiff finger, pointing out a line crudely drawn by the author. He didn't have to ask the question.

"I don't know what it means," Nigel confessed, "but I've seen it before. Somewhere."

"Well, think, Nigel. Think!"

The man's forehead wrinkled with thought. He stared blankly at Greg. His eyes didn't blink and reminded Greg of the cold, dead stare of a shark. For a second Greg imagined him probing inside his mind, seeking out all of his deep, dark, hidden secrets. It made him nervous to even think this man could read his thoughts. Greg pulled back from the table, unconsciously trying to escape the man's telepathic reach. In that instant, Greg heard the man laugh inside his mind. Greg closed his eyes and shook his head, refusing to let this force in. When he opened his eyes again and looked at Anguis, he saw a twinkle in his eyes.

"Now I know!" the man said.

"What? You know what?" Greg felt sick.

"Where I've seen this mark, of course."

"Oh. That." Greg started breathing again.

"Honestly, Mr. Moore, do you want to know or not?"

"Yes," Greg gave his head a shake and cleared his throat, "of course I do. Where *have* you seen this before?"

"Just down the street from here. At the House of Seven Gables. In the secret room," he whispered.

"There's a secret room?" Greg could feel his eyes widen, and immediately tried to narrow them.

"Tsk, tsk, tsk," the man shook his index finger back and forth. "Now, really, Mr. Moore, if you're going to uncover the past, you must first be willing to study Salem's history." The man sighed before going on. "During the infamous witch trials, the owner of the house had nieces whom he feared would be falsely accused of witchcraft, so he built a secret room to hide them in until the hysteria blew over. I know I've seen these same markings there."

Greg reached across the table and pulled the copies toward him. He slid the pages together and folded them carefully, peering under his shirt as he tucked them safely away. "Want to come along?" he asked, lifting his eyes to look at Nigel Anguis.

He was gone! In an instant he had disappeared without sound, just as he had come. Greg twisted in his seat and peered out the window. He searched the sidewalk for a glimpse of him, but somehow knowing deep in his gut he wouldn't find him.

The waitress came again to freshen his cup, and he must have looked a bit shaky as she asked him if he'd like a sandwich to go with his caffeine. He couldn't think of food. Not now.

"The man that was just here," Greg gestured, pointing to the opposite side of the table. "Did you see where he went?"

The waitress looked at him strangely. "Sir, I haven't see anyone at this table but you."

"That's ridiculous!" he raised his voice. People looked up from their tables and stared at him. He didn't care. He had to know. "I've been talking with him for the past half hour. What do you mean you haven't seen anyone at this table but me?" She looked at him with blank eyes, and he felt sick. "Never mind," he said, caressing his temples, "just give me the check."

"Sure thing, buddy," she said, slapping the check down on the table. She shook her head as she walked away, and from the expression on the faces of the couple that sat at the next table, Greg surmised she had rolled her eyes as she passed as if to say he was nuts. Maybe he was.

Greg stood and felt his legs go weak. He threw down a five and two ones on the table and shuffled toward the door and out of The Crystal Café. The heat hit him in the face like he'd just opened an oven door. He walked around the side of the building and untied Phoenix. Phoenix let out a wimpy whine and Greg knew the dog needed a drink. The reality of it snapped Greg out of the fog he was in, but didn't give him the courage to go back into the café, instead he promised Phoenix some water as they started down the street toward the House of Seven Gables.

Waves of heat danced over the pavement, penetrating the soles of his work boots. He should have gone back to his little hole-in-the-wall apartment and changed into something cooler, but he couldn't waste time. For all he knew Nigel Anguis had thrown him a curve ball and was now on his way to retrieve the coven's little black book for himself. Greg smiled slightly, patting his hip pocket. If old Nigel had only known he had the original on him during their meeting, maybe his story would have been different. Greg couldn't be sure. Perhaps the man was at this very moment searching his apartment for the scroll. Or perhaps, there wasn't a man at all. Shivers ran down his back, a strangely welcomed contrast to the heat.

When he entered the parking lot of the House of Seven Gables he walked amongst a small cluster of trees to his left. He tied Phoenix to a red maple, assuring he would be in the shade for the duration of his visit to the house. Phoenix was panting pretty heavily. Greg had to find him some water. He looked up and noticed a gardener's shed attached to the left side of the house. As he started walking toward it he saw a leaky spigot protruding from its side and a bucket beneath it to catch the drip. Upon closer inspection he saw the water was a little green with algae, so he dumped it out and drew a fresh pail and carried it back to Phoenix. As soon as Greg set the bucket down, Phoenix's head was in it. He drank nearly a third of it before laying down in the sparse grass beneath the shade tree.

"I'll be back soon, boy," he said, petting the dog's head. Phoenix only yawned, laying his snout down on his paws. He was content for the time being. Greg straightened and walked to the main entrance of the house and went inside.

The room was very small and crowded with school children waiting to take the tour. Greg made his way to the counter and bought a ticket, then moved to the side of the room with his back against the wall. It seemed an eternity, but finally a door opened to the left of the counter and a gray haired tour guide beckoned them to follow her. She led them from room to room explaining all the different artifacts, and when the entire group was standing in the formal dining room she said she had a surprise for everyone. She walked to the wall beside Greg and opened a hidden door. As she did, Greg's heart began to thud.

"This is a passage way that leads up to a secret room," she revealed. "Please watch your step as it is narrow and the stairs are uneven." She walked through the doorway and one by one the tour group made their way up the stairs.

The secret room was hardly large enough to hold them all. Greg stood with one foot still on the staircase, unable to see the entire room. The guide told them the story about the owner hiding his nieces in the room during the trials, but nothing about any mark in the room.

"If you'll all turn and carefully go back down the stairs, and wait for me in the room on the right, we'll continue our tour in just a few minutes," the gray haired lady said politely.

Greg stepped into the room and let the others pass him and start their descent. He waited until all that remained in the room was the tour guide and himself.

"I'm curious that you neglected to mention a strange mark that is said to be in this room," he said, pulling from his pocket the copy of the scroll. "Like this one." He held it so she could see only the mark. He watched her eyes light up and she smiled. He supposed she was surprised that anyone his age would even care.

"My Lord!" she chuckled. "How did you ever know about that? Very few guides have even seen it. It was found years ago during renovations. Some said it was drawn by someone who was hidden here during the onset of the witch trials, but there was never any proof found to collaborate the find. And then, of course, there were those that argued it was merely a carpenter's mark, so the Historical Society ruled it wouldn't be a showcase for the tourists. I must say, young man, you are the first to ever question me about it. It's quite refreshing really, to have such a knowledgeable visitor." She leaned in toward him and whispered with her hand covering half of her mouth, "We don't get that many around here." She giggled.

"Where is the mark? Can you show it to me?"

"Sure," she shrugged, "let me see if I can find it. It's been years since I've even thought of it." Turning to the slanted ceiling on the left side of the room, she looked around the backside of a beam. "Yup, here it is."

Greg took her place as she stepped back for him to see. It was exactly like the drawing on the scroll with the exception of three wavy lines to the right of the mark.

"We really have to join the others," she interrupted. "You know, I'm not supposed to leave them unattended."

"I won't tell," Greg smiled and gave her a wink. She smiled back at him and rolled her eyes toward the door. "I understand," Greg said reluctantly and lifted his right arm saying, "After you, dear lady." He watched her as she went out the door before him and thought of his dad and how he always said a little charm goes a long way.

"Oh my, so handsome *and* a gentleman," she chuckled.

Greg took one more, quick look at the room and followed her down the stairs. He didn't really hear much more of the rest of the tour, he was too busy thinking about what he had seen and what it all meant. *Could Ziea have been the one hiding in the secret room? Was it she who scratched the image in the wood*? The questions echoed in his mind as he followed the tour group out through the rear door of the house and into the hot, humid air. The guide led her audience off to the right toward a small building she said was once used to house the servants, but Greg had seen enough and parted their company. He walked through the back yard and down a dead end street toward the harbor and sat down at the edge of the ocean. He took a deep breath of the briny air and let it out slowly, trying to relax. Waves lapped at the pillars of a nearby pier, its rhythm unchanged by time. The ebb and flow were as his thoughts, neither coming nor going, but mingling and swirling as one idea flowed into another. He first looked across the ocean then down at the markings on the scroll. As he stared at the mark, his index finger unconsciously placed three wavy lines to the right of the drawing. Suddenly it hit him, and his eyes opened wide and his heart skipped a beat. The wavy lines were the ocean! It was a map! He'd bet his life on it. A laugh came out of him and was swallowed up by the sea, though nothing could steal his joy. He was going to find out where the map would lead him, but he needed help. He tried to quiet his pounding heart so that he could hear himself think, and in so doing, he remembered the surveyor back at the construction site. Perhaps he would have access to the type of map he needed.

He scrambled to his feet and jogged back to where he had left Phoenix tied to the tree. His fingers tugged at the knot in the rope and he cursed at it under his breath. On the one hand he knew he had to slow down and concentrate on the knot lest he pull the wrong end and tighten it more, and on the other hand he knew he had no time to waste. Nigel Anguis could very well be a step ahead of him. With that thought in mind, Greg pulled his jackknife out of his pocket and cut the rope. Phoenix yelped and pranced around, happy at last to be free from the tree.

"Come on, boy," he called to him and Phoenix walked swiftly beside Greg, his tail wagging back and forth behind him. After walking nearly three blocks up Derby Street, Greg finally was able to hail a cab, and then within minutes they were back at the construction site, and as luck would have it, the surveyor was still on the premises.

"Can you wait for me?" Greg asked the driver.

"Sure, but time is money, buddy."

"I'll make it worth your while."

"Then I can wait all day, son."

With that agreed, Greg hopped out of the cab, telling Phoenix to stay. He hustled over toward the buildings where he thought he had caught a glimpse of the surveyor.

"Walter!" Greg yelled above the whine of skill saws and the pop of nail guns.

"Hey, Greg, you decided to come back to work?" he bellowed.

"Not quite, Walt," he said, lowering his voice as they came closer to each other. "I need your expertise."

"How's that?" Walter scowled.

Greg showed him the drawing by Ziea. "Could this be a drawing of the shoreline here in Salem?"

"Well, let me have a closer look at this," he said as he put on his glasses and studied the odd shaped line. He hummed a little tune as he studied it and glanced at Greg every now and then, no doubt wondering what this was all about.

Greg held his breath and tried to stay cool while watching the guy rub the beard stubble on his chin and listening to him hum the same tune over and over again.

"Yeah," he said finally, causing Greg to jump. "I think I know where this is. But it ain't only Salem's shoreline."

"Huh?" Greg's face twisted into a grimace.

"Follow me into my office. I think I have just the map you're looking for."

Greg had all he could do to restrain himself from racing to the surveyor's trailer. Once inside he forced himself to stand patiently still while Walter searched through a file cabinet. Again the surveyor hummed.

"Ah, now here we go. I thought I still had this map in my files. Now, let's see if this strip map lines up with your drawing," Walter said, placing one beside the other. This time he whistled his little tune, blowing more air than sound. "Yup." He traced with his finger so Greg could follow along with what he was showing him. "The line in your drawing begins at Salem Harbor, then to Beverly Harbor, Castle Neck, Plum Island Sound, Kittery Point, and Casco Bay."

"Maine?"

"Yup. Looks like it ends at Sebasco Estates. See these two peninsulas right here?"

Greg leaned in closer for a better look. "Yeah, I think so. One says Bailey's Island and the other South Harpswell?"

"That's it. Well, this line curls directly to Sebasco."

"Are you sure? It's a crudely drawn line."

"Oh, but quite the contrary, it's very accurate. Whoever drew this must have had some knowledge of the geography of the shoreline. Too many likenesses to be coincidental. Check it out for yourself, my friend. It's all here in black and white."

Greg compared the two again. Had the scroll been as a clear overlay he was certain the lines would have matched perfectly with the surveyor's strip map. "Walter, you're a genius! I could give you a big fat juicy one about now." Greg grinned from ear to ear.

"Thanks, but no thanks. You know how the guys like to talk." He laughed.

"What do I owe ya, pal?"

"Ah, git outta here. You're stinkin' up the place." He smiled.

Greg quickly gathered up the scroll, threw open the door and skipped down the makeshift steps.

"Hey, what's this all about anyhow?" Walter shouted from the doorway of the trailer.

"No time to explain, the meter's running," Greg yelled back over his shoulder as he opened the back door of the cab, "but if things work out, I'll be back to take you out to the best meal money can buy. And, Walt, about the guys ... let them talk!"

"Okay, but I *refuse* to wear a dress," he yelled. Greg turned and blew him a kiss and Walter just grinned and shook his head as he closed the door to his office.

Greg slid into the back seat of the cab and grabbed the top of the front seat and pulled himself closer to the driver. Breathless from the excitement of what he had just learned, he told the driver to take him to the nearest bus station, then pushed himself back with both arms to sit beside Phoenix. The cabby calmly reached for the gearshift and put the car in drive. Finally the car began moving and pulled out of the lot. Greg's foot started tapping nervously on the floor as the cab driver puffed on a stubby, stale cigar and Phoenix panted in the seat beside Greg. Each puff and each pant seemed to Greg as a clock ticking off the seconds of an impending explosion. When they reached the bus station it was if someone had cut the correct wire just in time to preempt destruction. The car barely came to a stop as Greg scrambled out of the cab. He pulled Phoenix out by the leash and went to the front passenger side window to pay the driver. The cabby placed the soggy end of his cigar back in his mouth and grunted as he accepted his fee and sped off.

"*Now* he steps on it," Greg griped and waved the exhaust fumes away from his face. "Come on, boy, we've got a bus to catch." Phoenix barked and wagged his tail.

Greg counted his remaining cash and it turned out he had barely enough for his bus fare to Maine. He slipped the bus driver his last ten dollars to overlook Phoenix's presence. He still had his final paycheck in his pocket, so he wasn't going to let it bother him. There were more important things on his mind right now. Like getting to Sebasco Estates and beginning his search for the coven's Black Book. He watched every mile go by with Phoenix laying across his lap and thought he'd never hear the driver announce they had reached their destination. When the moment finally came, he stood on legs that had fallen asleep, and pins and needles shot through them as he stepped off the bus and onto Front Street in Bath, Maine.

The first person Greg met was an old gentleman seated on a bench under the awning of Wilson's Drug Store. Greg peered through the window and marveled at a scene from days gone by. There was an old fashioned soda fountain bar to the left with dozens of original Coca Cola glasses lined up on the shelves behind the bar and to the right a few small round tables with chairs, inviting passing patrons to rest their feet while enjoying a cool refreshment.

Greg looked back to the old gentleman that sat enjoying the day without a care in the world, it seemed to Greg. "Afternoon, Sir," he greeted him.

"Afternoon, to you, too, young fella," the man replied. He had a slow Down East fisherman's drawl. He braced back against the bench with his thumbs tucked under his suspenders. He wore a red and white plaid shirt with the edges of the collar frayed and the top pocket was torn, no doubt from years of holding the pipe that was sticking out of it.

"Can you tell me how to get to Sebasco Estates?" Greg asked him.

"Ayuh." He stretched out an arm and pointed up the street. "You go back thata way 'til you see the highway. You'll be on an overpass and there'll be a sign that says Phippsburg. You head right down that road and when you come to a 'Y' in the road, bare right. Other way goes to Popham Beach. Take that road straight down past the West Point Road and then there will be a left. That one takes you right down to the water. If you go by a little church and a graveyard, then you've gone too far and missed the road."

"Thank you very much, Sir," Greg said.

"Don't mention it, young fella." He hooked his thumbs back under his suspenders and nodded politely.

Greg tugged at Phoenix's leash and away they walked in the direction the old gentleman had pointed and about half an hour later they got lucky and hitched a ride in the back of a pickup truck. The closer they came to their destination, the more pungent the salty air became. Phoenix's nose was held high in the air as he sniffed and panted with excitement. The driver dropped them off at the road the old man said would take them down to the water's edge, and he and Phoenix walked the rest of the way.

The seaside village of Sebasco Estates was small. Greg counted only ten houses on his way down the narrow road that led to a seafood freezer plant at land's end. The plant's tin roof was white with gull droppings, and though to some that may have been a turn off, to Greg it seemed to render a bit of charm. A long wharf stretched out over the bay with a wire bushel basket hoist dangling from the end of a long wooden beam. A dragger with its hull full of fish was off loading its catch. Occasionally, the basket slammed into the pilings and spilled a few of the small fry into the water below that were immediately snatched up by the circling gulls overhead. Their cries sounded like laughter.

Greg walked to the water's edge and sat down on the rocky shoreline. The ledges glimmered with mica in the late afternoon sunshine. He admired a row of seaside cottages tucked snugly under the wings of the tall, gnarly pines. A small lobster boat was moored just off the shore, loaded down with wooden traps, each one containing a coil of rope and a red and black buoy. The thought of lobster made him realize just how hungry he was. With all the excitement he had forgotten to eat. Phoenix could probably use some chow, too.

"Hey boy, let's go into the plant's office and see if we can find out where to get something to eat around here," he said, slapping the side of his leg. Phoenix obediently came and stood by his side. He understood the word "eat."

On the way into the office Greg saw a faded sign in the window that read, "Summer Cottage Rentals: Inquire Within."

"Hey, today may be our lucky day, huh, boy?" Phoenix barked once and they went in.

Once inside, Greg saw the office was a variety store as well. Mostly canned goods, fishing bait, and supplies. He and Phoenix had made due with a whole lot less from time to time while on the road. A man sat behind a counter on a round bar stool, leaning over a newspaper, unconcerned that he had a customer. A fisherman, Greg presumed to be the captain of the dragger, stuck his head through the doorway, that led out to the pier. He smelled of fish and gasoline, and wore a dark green chamois shirt with the sleeves rolled up and its tail hanging out over his dingy blue jeans. His hip boots were rolled down just below his knees, and one knee protruded through a hole with a few white threads drawn tightly across it.

"The load weighed up to forty-two hundred, Sid. Just apply it to my tab," he told the old man seated on the stool.

"Ayuh, will do, Forrest," he replied, not taking his eyes off the newspaper.

Greg watched the fisherman leave, then he stepped up to the counter and cleared his throat. Still the man didn't look up. "Excuse me," Greg said.

An unfamiliar voice finally got the man's attention and he looked up suddenly. "Yes, sir, what can I do ya fer?"

"I'm looking to rent one of those cottages," Greg told him, pointing to the sign in the office window. "Maybe for what's left of the summer and some of the fall. Depends on whether or not I find what I'm looking for around here."

"Well, if it ain't an achin' back, hungry belly, and a wet behind, you've come to the wrong place, sonny."

Greg laughed. "I think I like it here already."

"To each his own, young man." He placed a finger

to his lips. "Now, let me see, I think the Wilson's place is empty. It's sparsely furnished, but the roof don't leak."

"I'll take it … provided you can cash my check," Greg added. He removed the check from his pocket and placed it on the counter in front of the man.

"Sure. Seems like a waste of hard earned cash if you ask me, but it's your dime. The Wilson place is the dark green cottage with the white trim. Third one down the shore," he said and pointed in its direction.

"Great. What do I owe you for … say … two months' rent?"

"Oh, how does $650.00 sound?"

"Like a bargain!" Greg said with a smile.

"That's what you say now. You haven't seen the place yet," he joked. He then opened a metal index card box and pulled out a key. "Here ya go. Just be sure and return it when you leave." He placed the key in Greg's hand.

"I'll do that. Thank you."

"Anything else I can do ya fer?"

"I'll need some food for myself and my dog."

"Help yourself to what I have. I think you'll find the prices reasonable."

"And a phone?" Greg looked around, leaning back to peer between aisles in order to see the wall at the back of the store.

"Down on the pier there's a phone. Coastguard regs, you know."

"Thanks," he said, and turned to walk down the

aisle to gather some groceries.

"Don't mention it. Glad to be of service to ya," the man said as he turned the page on his newspaper and smoothed it out on the counter top.

Greg picked up enough food to last him a few days. Perhaps he'd be able to get a ride into town to shop for more of a variety. All the small store had were cans of Alpo, and Phoenix couldn't stay on a diet of that for too many days before it would give him the runs. He paid the old gentleman and he and Phoenix went out the door.

As they left, Greg noticed a sign in the window of a house across the street. It read, "Visions of Valkner–Fortunes Told."

"Alright!" Greg said to Phoenix. "I'll have to come back and check that place out." Phoenix answered with a bark. At times Greg thought the dog could understand what he was saying.

He hurried along now that he knew he had entertainment to look forward to, wrestling with the grocery bag in one arm and Phoenix on his leash tugging on the other arm. They walked the narrow path that wove along the shoreline and soon they stood in front of a dark green cottage with white trim.

"This must be it, Phoenix. Home." He reached down and removed the dog's leash. Phoenix wagged his tail and ran to the front door. As Greg approached the cottage he wiggled a hand into the front pocket of his jeans and removed the key. He slipped it into the lock and turned it, then gave the door a gentle shove and it swung open. For a moment Greg thought the rusty hinges screeched his name. It made the hairs on the back of his neck stand up, and he almost took a step backward, but he shook it off and stepped inside. Phoenix wasn't a bit spooked. He trotted right in and jumped up on an old tattered brown loveseat, and made himself at home.

Dust swirled in the beam of light coming from the doorway, and the room was stuffy and stale smelling from the lack of ventilation. He set the groceries down on a small dinette table just inside the door and went to the bay window that faced the ocean. Kneeling on the wooden window seat, he pushed open the wooden shutters and let in the first cross breeze the place had had in a long time.

With the increased light he was getting a better look around. There was a small bathroom with a manual flush toilet and a three pound coffee can in the corner half full of various brands of cigarette butts. The place was definitely rustic. It was built with rough cut lumber and no wall board had ever been installed. The walls were covered with pictures that had been cut out of magazines and pasted on haphazardly. At first glance one might think it was a psycho's pad, but upon closer inspection it was most probable that the mélange was the work of partying college brats. Even two columns that stretched from floor to ceiling were covered with pictures. These particular photos weren't the kind of snapshots you'd send home to mother. They bordered on pornography. Greg smiled at himself as he thought of giving them a closer inspection a bit later. Right now he had to divert his attention to his growling belly.

He checked out the kitchen area, which consisted of one badly scratched ceramic sink with an empty tin basin in it, a small side board complete with a manual water pump for drawing water from the well, and one cupboard, its door ajar, revealing an empty box of Cracker Jacks and an old poker for removing the burner covers on the potbellied stove that sat in the middle of the main room.

He thought about checking around for some wood, but the pangs in his empty stomach wouldn't allow it. He'd just open a can of Spaghettios and eat them cold. That's when he thought again of his sister—cold Spaghettios always grossed her out. He wondered what she was going to say about all of this, and suddenly he didn't feel so hungry.

He emptied nearly the whole bag of groceries before finding the can opener. As soon as he started turning its metal handle, Phoenix jumped down from the loveseat and came to stand beside Greg with his tail wagging happily back and forth. He opened three small cans of Alpo and scooped them out into the tin wash basin with a plastic spoon. He carried it over to the loveseat with Phoenix right at his heels, and sat it down on the floor. The dog acted like he hadn't eaten for a week as he pressed his muzzle hard against the side of the dish to allow himself the largest mouthful he could swallow. He finished in no time and Greg filled the basin with water. Phoenix drank half of the water before coughing a couple of times and then curling up on the floor at Greg's feet. Full and sleepy, he didn't even flinch as Greg got up off the loveseat and scuffed across the floor to the door and out of the cottage. He could do with some sleep himself, but first he had to see if the fortune teller was still open for business. His sister had accused him of wasting more money on so-called psychics that he would never live it down, but it made no matter, he couldn't pass up the chance to check it out, after all, this one could be the real McCoy. Again she would say that was what he always told himself as he threw his money into the wind, but he didn't care. He hadn't come this far to stop now, so he continued down the pathway with his sister's words echoing in his mind, and raised a finger just to test the direction of the wind.

The tide was at ebb, and the air was thick with the aroma of the muddy clam flats that reached into the sea. He could taste the salt in the air as he plowed through the overgrowth and stepped out onto the cleared path. The sun was low, behind the row of trees that towered over the cottages, and he hoped the fortune teller would still be open and would have a flashlight he could borrow to find his way back.

As he neared the end of the path he could hear the continuous hum of the conveyor belt as it carried the fish from the end of the pier to the freezer. A radio inside the plant blared an old tune, and a few of the workers bellowed the lyrics to the chorus of "Hotel California" by the Eagles. Their voices nearly drowned out the motors on the machines, the cry of the sea gulls, and the slicing of fish. It reminded Greg of the old movies about the chain gangs of the oppressed south.

Once he stepped into the dirt parking lot at land's end he could see the sign in the window at the fortune teller's shop. It still read, "Open," so he walked up the slow incline and went inside. A clanking cow bell over the door announced his entry, but no one came to greet him. The room was small and jam packed with all sorts of occult paraphernalia. A counter with an antique cash register was at the back of the room and to its left was a doorway covered by a beaded curtain.

"Hello, is anybody here?" Greg called into the back room. He listened, but no answer. Perhaps the fortune teller was busy with a client. He didn't know, but felt it could be worth the wait, so he occupied himself by checking out the shop and fantasizing about selling his find to the owner. He turned his back to the beaded curtain and busied himself with studying an antique Ouija board. Suddenly, the beaded curtain parted and the fortune teller stepped through the doorway. It startled Greg and he spun around to come eye to eye with him.

The man was about sixty years old, Greg surmised, with thinning gray hair and a big, bushy mustache that covered his upper lip entirely. He wore a pair of small round wire rimmed glasses that were slid down on his nose, forcing him to peer over the tops of the frames. If it wasn't for the black smock he wore with the golden signs of the zodiac printed all over it, Greg would have never guessed that this man was the fortune teller. That, and one other thing. The man's eyes. It seemed to Greg that this man was looking straight through his physical body and into a place that no one had ever seen. With their eyes still locked on to each other, the man spoke, with his face only inches from Greg's.

"Go home, son, before it's too late," he warned Greg.

"Hey, I just got here," he said and then he smiled, but it was a forced, nervous smile. "How much for a reading?" Greg took out his wallet and began to open it, but the man placed his hand over it, preventing him from doing so.

"I have nothing to tell you, except, go home, now," he said, then turned to walk away. Greg caught his arm and turned him around to face him again. The man couldn't hide his reaction. His eyes told on him. He was afraid.

"What has you so shaken, old man?" Greg was

beginning to feel nervous himself. None of the other fortune tellers ever pulled this act on him. He wasn't about to let this old man get to him. "What gives?"

"Look, son, what I see isn't written in stone. You have the power to change the future, but you must leave now, before you uncover something that will change all of our lives."

"Oh, sure, I get it now," Greg nodded. "Tell me something, old man, how much did Nigel Anguis pay you to throw a scare into me?"

"You're wrong about him, son. He *wants* you to find what you're looking for."

"And how would you know that? Oh wait, of course, because you're 'the seer of all things,' right?" Greg pointed at the sign in the window.

"Only some things, son," he said, dropping his eyes. "Some things I wish not to see."

Greg shook his head, sorry he'd ever left the cottage, and quickly made his way for the door. The fortune teller came after him and caught him by his shirt sleeve as Greg was reaching for the door handle.

"The Dark Dragon has met you, son. I had hoped you would listen, but in my soul I knew you would not." He placed a card in Greg's pocket. "Take this, boy, if you're lucky, and I'm wrong, just maybe you'll get to call me. I don't know what I'll be able to do to help you, but I'll try."

Greg yanked away from the man. "Old coot," he said angrily as he bolted out the door.

He walked toward the pier, trying to shake off the bad vibes he had gotten from the old man. He wasn't about to let anything stand in his way of fame. Certainly not the ramblings of a-wanna-be psychic. He needed to talk to someone with both feet on the ground, and suddenly he really wanted to talk with his sister. Maybe she could relieve his tension.

He found the phone about halfway out on the pier and dialed her number, only to be disappointed when he got her answering machine again. He waited patiently for her recorded greeting to finish playing then he spoke into the phone. He was even more disturbed when he heard his voice was shaky. He cleared his throat and began again.

"Hey, Sis, it's me again. I'm in Sebasco Estates, Maine, by a seafood freezer plant. I've got a cottage here for the next couple of months, but I don't think I'll be here for that long at all. I've already met the un-welcoming committee. Tomorrow I'm hiking up along the shoreline and once I find what I'm looking for, I'm outa here. I'll call again next Friday as planned. The vultures will be out when they discover the nature of my find, but not to worry, Sis, I can handle the competition. Love you. Bye." He hung up the phone, feeling empty. For once, he really wanted to talk to her. He needed to hear her tell him to not believe in all the psychic mumbo jumbo.

He got back to the cottage about nine o'clock, and Phoenix was waiting by the door when he walked in. "Sorry to leave you, boy," he said as he petted the dog's head. "Tomorrow you can go with me." Greg let him out to relieve himself and Phoenix wasted no time lifting his leg on a nearby bush and then ran back inside. Greg laid down on the loveseat with his feet dangling over one end, and fell asleep with Phoenix sitting beside him, his head resting on Greg's thigh.

Morning came quickly and the sun's rays burst through the bay window, waking Greg as the light hit his face. It took him a minute to remember where he was, then he got up and went into the kitchen area. He opened a bottle of Sunny Delight and took a long drink, then he opened a can of Spaghettios and filled the void in his stomach. He splashed some water on his face, then he and Phoenix walked out of the door of the cottage and began their journey along the shoreline.

He walked not knowing really what he was looking for. Was it going to be a building? A cave? An ancient alter? He didn't know. But he was prepared to search every square inch of land in Sebasco Estates if need be to find the coven's final resting place. After his little meeting with the fortune teller the night before, he was positive he was close to making his dreams come true. *Or ... nightmares.* A chill ran up his back.

Phoenix ran ahead of him, sniffing every pile of rotten seaweed he came upon. Suddenly, he stopped and sat staring into the woods. Greg caught up to him and was surprised to hear a deep growl coming from his throat. He had never heard Phoenix growl like that before.

"What's the matter, boy?" Greg spoke gently to him. Phoenix just lowered his head and continued to growl. His body was shaking.

Greg turned his head and looked in the same direction as Phoenix was looking. There, set back in a thicket of overgrown brush was an old stone shelter. Greg's heart began to pound and he took a deep breath and tried to calm himself. It could be nothing, but his gut had become a knot.

"Let's check it out, boy," he said as he began to

weave his way through the thorn bushes and vines. Phoenix wouldn't move. He just sat there on his haunches and continued to growl. "You're no help," Greg called back to him, then he mumbled to himself, "Couldn't have found a pit bull that day in Phoenix, could I? Nah, I had to find a German shepherd. A spineless German shepherd." He turned his back to glance at Phoenix and walked the rest of the way to the building.

As he stood in front of the stone shelter, it was obvious the place had been empty for years. Vines had grown across the front of the building and Greg had to cut them away with his jack knife. He pushed the door open and stood there looking in. He had to force himself to fold up his knife and put it back into his pocket. He told himself that he was being ridiculous, after all, it was obvious the place was deserted.

He stepped inside and was surprised that despite the hot summer day, the building had kept its chill. The air was stale even though several stones in the shelter walls had been knocked out years ago. Dead leaves littered the floor, and the only furniture remaining was a cot that Greg imagined had long since been ripped apart by raccoons and other small animals. He searched the entire shelter and was disappointed that he found nothing to suggest the coven had been there. He turned to leave and as he crossed one area of the floor it seemed to give a little under his feet. He stopped in his tracks and bent down. Brushing away dirt and leaves that had accumulated over the years, he found there was a two foot square section of floor that could be lifted out. He opened the hatch and peered down into a black hole. All he could see was a vertical ladder reaching down to a dirt floor.

He shook with excitement. *Could this be it? Could he have found the coven's final resting place so easily?* He tried to calm himself as he thought about the fortune teller and what he had said about Anguis wanting him to find it. He felt weak in the knees, but he found the courage to climb down the ladder and into the black hole.

He stood on the dirt floor and lit a match, illuminating a huge dugout room. Slowly he turned, taking it all in, until the flickering light shined on a crude built alter. His heart nearly leaped out of his chest when he saw a dust covered black book. A slow, deliberate laugh escaped from his throat and escalated into a wild "yahoo!" The match burned down and burnt his finger. He dropped the match and shook his hand, then stuck his finger in his mouth to cool the burn. Not letting the pain ruin his moment of joy, he reached into his pocket and took out the book of matches. In the dark, he fumbled with the match book until he got it open and tore off another match. He struck it three times before it finally caught fire and blazed like a torch in the dugout room. The altar appeared again in front of him and the book lay there like an open invitation. Greg pounced on the book and drew it to his chest, laughing hysterically. With the book held tightly in his left hand and the lit match in the other, he spun on his heels to leave the dugout and found his face inches from the face of Mary Deven!

She reached out a clawed hand and ripped his Adam's apple from his throat while the match still smoldered between his fingers. With the second swipe she sliced the front of his torso and his stomach contents spilled out onto the dirt floor. Greg was amazed of how time stood still as he looked down and saw the puddle of Spaghettios at his feet. In his mind, he laughed a little as he looked at how many of the macaroni circles remained whole. *He could have sworn he chewed his food better than that.* The light began to fade and Greg dropped on his knees. Mary and Sarah Deven were on him at once as they threw him to the dirt floor like a rag doll and gorged themselves on his warm blood. Then darkness came.

*Then thou spakest in a vision to thy holy
one, and saidst, I have laid help upon one that is
mighty; I have exalted one chosen out of the people.*

Psalm 89:19

CHAPTER 5–THE SUMMONS

Peter sat on a black leather sofa in Deke's office with his elbows resting on his knees and his face buried in his hands. He'd be the first to admit that he needed a rest, but he just couldn't stop watching. His fingers parted and he peered through them and stared at the TV screen once again. Each time he played the tape of Roberto Sanchez sitting there on that old ratty sofa, staring at him with those yellow eyes and that smile of absolute evil, he couldn't help but feel he'd met this demon before.

Memories flooded his mind, taking him back to the days in New York when he worked for the debunking organization. He had been teamed with a professor from a prestigious college university who was supposed to help keep his feet planted firmly on the ground. Little did they know what the power of persuasion and a little experience in unexplainable phenomena could do to a man. He remembered one time in particular. A time he wished he could forget.

They had been called out in the middle of the night to an apartment in a small town near Buffalo, New York. Even as he reminisced he could feel the tightness in his chest that he had felt that night, walking that long, graffiti covered hallway to the apartment door. He could taste the soured bile that had come up in his throat when the door opened and he looked into that sweet lady's desperate eyes. Eyes that begged for help. Much like Maria Rosario's eyes as she had begged him to help her brother.

"Please, help my Michael!" she cried, and led them into a small bedroom. They stood, frozen in the entryway with their eyes turned to the ceiling. The boy, twelve years old, had levitated to the top of the room, his chest nearly crushed between the ceiling and the supernatural force that held him there. His face was turned toward them with his right cheek pressed hard against the ceiling. A white, misty cloud of plaster swirled in the room beneath him, creating the illusion of him floating in a cloud.

The woman grabbed each of them by the cuffs of their suit coats and dragged them further into the room, and begged them to help her son. She screamed for them to get him down as the white plaster dust cascaded down around them and coated their bodies with a blood tinged powder. The labored breathing of the boy filled the room as he sucked in short, wheezy gasps of air. From blue lips came a voice of many demons, and with barely enough breath to speak, he cursed God.

Peter had looked squarely into the eyes of the professor that night, and without a word said to him, *"See? See? I told you there were things in the darkness. I told you."* And for that brief moment when their eyes met, he was sure the professor heard every word. He would never forget the look on his face as he watched his world of logic crumble. There was no triumph in unveiling his misconceptions, and Peter would have given most anything for the professor to have been able to explain it all away that night. But it wasn't to be so. Not then, and not now.

Peter tried to shake the memory from his mind and snatched up the remote control and pushed the pause button. It froze on a frame of Sanchez's face. The glowing, yellow eyes glared from the screen, and a knot formed in the pit of Peter's stomach that churned like molten rock. He had looked into those eyes before. He wanted so badly to be wrong. To not have to go through that hell again. But a voice, somewhere within the forbidden, dark cavities of his mind, spoke to him, saying, *"It's been a long time, Peter. Let's play."* That voice scared him. It was the voice that had come from that little boy in that sweet lady's apartment. The same voice that came from Roberto Sanchez.

Peter was so involved with the video that he didn't realize Deke had come into the office. It wasn't until he sat down beside him on the sofa and the cushions deflated a loud puff of air, that he was fully aware of his presence.

"Pretty incredible stuff, huh, Pete?" Deke was one of those people that never shut up. He was always the guy at the movies that sat right in front of you, talking during the whole movie. Peter just ignored him, as he didn't seem to require an answer. "Are you feeling better yet?"

He reached into a can of mixed nuts that was on the side table on a stack of old tabloid newspapers and popped a handful in his mouth. "I guess you being a 'sensitive' and all, it really hit you pretty hard." He chuckled.

"There's something about this, Deke," he said, ignoring Deke's snide remarks. "I feel everything is somehow connected. My past, Sanchez, and even the dreams I've been having."

"Huh?" Deke asked with his mouth full of nuts. A row of freckles across his forehead disappeared in a furrow as he scowled and looked sideways at Peter.

"Dreams. Visions." Peter sighed, hung his head and gave it a shake. "I don't know what they are, I just know they scare the crap out of me, because if it is all tied together, we're dealing with something really powerful here."

"Well, hot damn!" Pieces of nuts flew from his mouth. He slapped Peter on the back as he scooted off the sofa and scrambled around his desk to pick up the phone.

"Who are you calling?" Peter finally turned from the screen to look at Deke.

"The program manager," he said, dialing the numbers. "We're going to need a larger time slot next week."

Peter jumped to his feet and grabbed the phone from Deke and slammed it back into its cradle. "What do you think this is, you idiot! A game? Haven't you heard anything I've been saying to you? What's happening here is real, Deke, you can bet your life on that, but it's not something that's going to happen when you want it to so as to fit it neatly into a scheduled time slot that some big shot producer wants filled on Halloween night! Take it from me, Deke, there are some things that lay sleeping that you don't want to awaken, because if you do they just might jump up and bite you on the ass!"

"Well," Deke exhaled and rolled his eyes, "pardon me for trying to do my job, Pete." Then he bent over his desk and stared Peter down, his face only a couple of inches from his. "You'd do well to take the example from me. You're going to learn, you can't fight with the big boys."

"Yeah? Well, watch me," Peter said. He stormed out of Deke's office and slammed the door behind him. He could hear Deke swearing at him through the door, calling him every dirty name in the book. That was okay. He'd forgive Deke. He couldn't possibly understand what he was up against, and Peter thought it should stay that way. Maybe then, Deke would be safe.

Peter drove away from Deke's office and headed back to his hotel. It would have been easy for some to keep going at this point. To keep driving until they had run out of roads and away from all the madness. But not for Peter. There was a familiar tug in his belly that wouldn't let him leave. A tug that told him that evil was at hand. He had learned over the years to pay attention to the tug. Some called him a psychic. He hated that classification. It made him feel like he was part of the darkness, playing the devil's games. The professor had convinced him on more than one occasion to fight fire with fire, but Peter wasn't comfortable around Ouija boards and Tarot cards. His Bible was his sword. His faith the healer of his wounds. But at the same time, he knew that God sometimes worked in mysterious ways, and so from time to time he humored the professor and was surprised to find they had become quite a team, traveling all over the United States and helping those that the church and the debunking organization had refused.

It wasn't long after Peter had left the organization that the professor called and told him that he, too, had been relieved of further services. Since that time, the professor, still very much involved in parapsychology, would stumble upon those in need of help, and would call Peter for assistance. Sadly, he dreaded receiving calls from his endeared friend. A call meant evil had found him again.

Peter stepped up to the front desk of the hotel and tapped his fingers on the counter top to get the clerk's attention. This time the guy sat with his face only inches from a six inch portable TV watching the San Diego Chargers beat the pants off the 49ers.

"Excuse me, but would you have another room pass key for me? I think I must have left mine in my room."

He looked up and saw Peter. "Mr. Amado," he greeted him, then reached into a bag of nachos and shoved them into his mouth. "Sorry, but I haven't ..."

"...had a thing to eat all day." Peter finished the sentence for him and smiled.

"Ah, yeah, right." The clerk brushed his hand off on the side of his trousers and picked up a stack of pages torn from a memo pad. He slid them across the counter to Peter. "Your messages, sir," he said snidely. "All from Mr. Crandell." He rolled his eyes as he turned and reached for another pass key. "Anything else I can do for you, sir?"

Peter took the key and the messages. "I think I'm all set now, thank you."

He might have been put off by the clerk's attitude had he not known firsthand how impatient Deke Crandell could be. He'd have to call him, if only to give the kid behind the hotel desk a break, but first he was going to take a hot shower. It would do Deke good to stew a bit longer.

He opened the door to his room, walked to the bed and threw the pass key and the messages down on the side table. Then he went into the bathroom and turned on the shower. He stripped, opened the shower door, and stepped into the cloud of steam. He stood there letting the water rain over him, trying to rid himself of the feeling that something horrible was about to happen. It was the same feeling he had when he had walked down the hall to that small apartment outside of Buffalo. The same feeling he had as he had sat beside Roberto Sanchez, and later when he stood at the foot of the man's bed. The same feeling he always had after the dream. It was all connected. He knew it. He felt it. But how?

He got out of the shower and wrapped a towel around his waist. With the circular swipe of his hand, he wiped the steam off the mirror and stood there staring into his own deep blue eyes hoping to find some reason, but there were no answers to be found there. Suddenly, he felt old and tired. He reached up and rubbed the dark stubble on his face. The right side of his upper lip curled up in a snarl. He didn't feel in the mood to shave. Clicking off the bathroom light, he sauntered over to the bed and laid down on his back and looked up at the ceiling. He hated this time. It was always a time of impending disaster. The not knowing about what was going to happen, yet knowing full well it was going to be big. Like the calm in the eye of a storm.

The sun's reflection off a passing car flashed across the room, and for an instant Peter thought he saw that little boy smeared across the ceiling of his hotel room. The sight caught him by surprise and he drew in a sharp breath. He squeezed his eyes shut, and when he opened them again the image was gone. He laid there, breathing rapidly, wondering if he would ever be free from the horror of that night. Then he felt *the tug*.

It first started as a tickle in his belly, then turned to a feeling of dread that was so powerful he wanted to vomit. His head turned to look at the phone on the bedside table. He *knew* it was about to ring. Still, he jumped half out of his skin and sat bolt upright on the edge of the bed when its ring broke the silence of the room. He stared at it, hoping it would stop. He thought, if a person was to apply logic as to who might be on the other end when he lifted the receiver, one would have to suggest, in all probability, Deke Crandell. But Peter *knew* it was not. His gut was telling him different. He knew answering it was going to open a new door in his life. A door he wished he could keep shut. Slowly, with a will that seemed not to be his own, he lifted the receiver to his ear.

"Peter? Is that you?" A familiar voice both delighted and depressed him. It was the professor.

"Yeah, it's me," he answered. His heart was in his throat. He could hear the pause in the professor's voice, then the words came.

"It's found us, Peter. I've seen it in the eyes of a young man."

Peter could no longer hear what the professor was saying, as the proclamation had catapulted him into a vision of absolute horror. Where eternity and reality meet.

He was traveling within his own mind to a place he'd never seen. His hotel room vanished before his eyes and he found himself walking in a surreal world, with sound, color, and light. Forms were taking shape ahead of him. It was a man and his dog, walking along a rocky shoreline. Peter could taste the salty air and hear the gulls crying overhead. His legs felt heavy, as if he was in a dream, when he tried to catch up to the man. Just as he got close enough to place a hand on the man's shoulder, there was a flash of light and in that instant they were both transported to a dark, musty room, and they were not alone.

Peter stood as an observer behind the man, waiting for him to turn around, that he might see the man's face and learn the purpose of this vision, but as the man turned, a black cloud passed through Peter and encompassed the entire figure of the man. Peter couldn't see his face. Then, a loud clap of thunder brought Peter back to reality.

He sat on the edge of his hotel bed with sweat beading on his forehead. He still had a firm grip on the phone and it pressed hard against his left ear. At first the sounds were vague, but soon he was becoming more aware of the professor's voice coming through the receiver.

"Huh?" Peter shook his head.

"I said, you are needed, Peter. I am sure of it. Will you come?"

The door was open. He couldn't stop what was to happen now even if he wanted to. It had begun. His answer tore at his insides as it came up and out of him, committing himself to things unseen.

"I'll be on the next flight." Without another word, he lowered the phone and placed it gently in the cradle. He knew his old friend was right. *It* had found them again.

CHAPTER 6–IN THE MIND'S EYE

Tyler Moore stepped out of an Avis rental car and quickly closed the door. She pressed the entire length of her lean, tanned body against the side of the car as a huge white paneled truck barreled on past her. It had *"Fresh Seafood"* written in bold red script across the rear doors and a noisy freezer generator over the top of the cab. Its brakes squealed as it approached the wharf and scared up a flock of cackling sea gulls at land's end.

Tyler glanced up to see the driver's reflection in the passenger side mirror. His lips formed the word "Wow!", then puckered up and threw her a kiss. She looked away at once from his gaze, not wanting to draw any more attention. It was the same reaction she got most everywhere she went. Her brother, as well as her fellow photographers back at the magazine headquarters in New York, had always insisted she had missed her calling. They felt she should be in front of the camera instead of doing the pictorial layouts, but modeling was not her thing. She had never thought herself to be pretty, although she had always thought of her brother–her twin, no less–as being rather handsome.

Her brother. The reason she had come to Maine. It had been three weeks since she had gotten his last message left on her answering machine, and her face, despite her beauty, couldn't hide her worry. The more time that went by the harder it was for her to tell herself that he was alright, just goofing off, or shacked up with some fisherman's daughter. The more time that went by the more she thought about what he had said about meeting the "un-welcoming committee" and how the "vultures would be out when they discovered the nature of his find." Even as she stood in the afternoon sunshine, a shiver shot through her. *What had her brother gotten himself into this time?*

Another big truck was coming. She could feel the vibrations through the ground, and hear the engine's gears shift in the distance. She looked over the roof of the car at the wharf's office and spotted a cottage rental sign in the window. She hurried around the front of the car just as the big truck went whizzing by, its air brakes whispering, "*Chsh.*"

She pulled open the office door and went inside, stopping abruptly as she stepped over the threshold. The office/store was small to say the least, and small places always made her feel uneasy. For five years she had been with the magazine, working out of an office on the seventh floor, and had used the elevator only twice. She liked to tell herself–and others–that stair climbing was part of her workout routine. But she knew differently.

"Hello? Is anybody here?" she called out, peering over shelves of fishing gear, canned goods, and potato chips.

"Yes, Ma'am." A voice came from behind a counter that was cluttered with everything from nylon netting for lobster pots to little square plastic boxes of Mexican Jumping Beans.

Tyler made her way through the maze of grocery shelves and stepped up to the counter. "I'm looking for my brother, Gregory Moore. He said he rented a cottage near here. Did he by any chance rent it from you?"

"Ayuh, that he did, 'bout three or four weeks ago. Paid up for a couple months," he drawled.

Tyler let out a sigh of relief. "Can you direct me to the cottage?"

"Sure thing, Missy. You go down to the shore and you'll see a path that goes along the ledges. Stay on that path and his place is the third one you come to."

"Oh, thank you!" she said and hurried out the door.

"Hey," he yelled, "ask him what he's using for wood in the cookin' stove. He hasn't been in here to buy any. He'd better not be cuttin' on private property, folks 'round here don't take a likin' to that."

Tyler raised one arm in the air and waved it, signaling she had heard his warning, then lowered it slowly, the smile vanishing from her face. She tried telling herself that Greg was probably just being lazy and eating bologna sandwiches and cold canned goods, but that didn't stop her from hastening her steps and counting off the cottages as she went down the seaside path. Finally, the third cottage came into view. Its forest green siding blended into the pines. It was quiet. Too quiet. Tyler hustled up the steps and tried the door. It was unlocked.

"Greg, are you here?" she called out to him. Her blue-green eyes widened as she listened for an answer. There was none. Hesitantly, she stepped inside, leaving the door open. "Greg," she called out again. Still no answer.

She walked slowly around the room, trying to take it all in. There were so many pictures on the walls that it made it hard to separate the cottage's clutter from her brother's, but finally she spotted a familiar object. Phoenix's leash. Her heart began to beat normally again. She couldn't imagine Greg taking Phoenix too far without that leash. He always hated it when other people just let their dogs run loose. Maybe he had just gone out for a while. She'd tidy the place up a bit and kill some time. Surely he'd be back soon. She sighed, smiled, and shook her head, and wondered how two people whose appearance was so alike, could be so different.

She picked up the wash basin beside the loveseat and carried it into the small kitchen area. An empty grocery bag sat on the counter, and beside it several cans of dog food, a can of Dinty Moore Beef Stew, a jug of Sunny Delight, and three cans of Spaghettios, one of which had been opened. She slowly pulled herself closer to the counter and forced herself to look into the open can. The air suddenly became thinner, and she struggled to breathe. The leftovers in the bottom of the can had dried to the point that the little "o"s were stretched out to the side of the can as if they were in some sort of space warp. He had been gone longer than just a little while.

Tyler backed out of the small kitchen and threw her purse down on the loveseat. Frantically she searched the room for clues of his whereabouts. There seemed to be none, then she found something. A business card lay on the floor staring up at her. She snatched it up so quickly that she barely noticed she had broken a nail.

"Visions of Valkner–Fortunes Told," she read aloud. The corners of her mouth stretched into a smile. "Of course, Tyler, you idiot," she said to herself, "he's probably camped out on the fortune teller's floor, for God's sake."

She grabbed her purse off the loveseat and ran out of the cottage with the card still clutched in her hand. She was already loading the artillery, forming in her mind just what she was going to say to him for worrying her this way. And so help him if he came up with some lame excuse, she was going to bop him one. Something she hadn't done since they were kids.

She came to the end of the path and had to wait for yet another truck to turn around before she could check out the buildings across the street from the wharf. She wanted to yell at the driver, to tell him that she had better things to do than to just stand there while he ogled her, but she didn't. She knew from past experience that this would only give him a reason to stop and try to make conversation. Right now, the only one she wanted to talk to was her brother.

The truck pulled away, at last, and gave her a clear view of the fortune teller's shop. She stuffed the card in her pocket and angrily strutted across the narrow street and into the quaint little shop. An old cow bell clanged above the door and she reached up and stopped it from ringing.

"Come in, come in," a muffled voice invited her.

At first she couldn't see from whom the voice came, then she saw the man, but from only the waist down. The rest of him was bent over a huge packing crate.

"Please, feel free to look around," he told her. "I just got a delivery of some antique items that I simply must check for damage."

"That's quite alright. I'll wait," she said. Even she could hear the disappointment in her voice. Her brother wasn't there.

The old man grunted, seeming to be having a hard time with reaching the bottom of the wooden crate. Tyler walked up behind him and tried to get a glimpse of the rest of the old gentleman and perhaps of what all was left in the huge box. "Do you need some help?" she asked. She bobbed from side to side, trying to get a better look.

"Perhaps you could do one small thing for me, Miss," he grunted.

"Sure."

"Grab my belt with both hands and pull for all you're worth."

"Well," she said under her breath, "I've never had it put to me in quite that way before, but okay." She wiggled her hands under the old man's belt and yanked him back good and hard.

The old man came up and out of the crate and they stumbled backwards. Tyler thought they were both going down on the floor, but thanks to her height, she was able to step back far enough to give the old man room to twirl around and face her. He was looking at her strangely as she watched the color drain from his face. "Are you alright?" she asked. He wasn't answering. "I'm looking for ..."

"Your brother?" he asked.

Tyler whipped her head around to look at the sign in the fortune teller's window. "Damn, you *are* good!" They both laughed.

"I must admit, I can't take the credit for this one. It's the resemblance."

"Then you've seen him! Thank God." She let out a big sigh of relief as the old man nodded. "He's my twin," she needlessly told him. She couldn't help herself. She always rambled on when she was excited. "His name is Gregory. Gregory Moore. I'm Tyler." She offered to shake his hand.

The fortune teller pulled his eyes away from hers. "You shouldn't have come here."

"Is that what you told my brother?" she asked. Her voice was rigid.

"Words to that effect. Who's the fortune teller now?" he said snidely.

"My, but you have gotten grumpy all of a sudden. Maybe I should have left you hanging upside down in that old crate," she fumed.

"Not only do you look like him, but you've got the temper to match," he mumbled with his back to her.

"I'm sorry. I'm not usually like this, but I'm getting worried about him. It's been ..."

"Three weeks," the old man finished her sentence. "It's been three weeks since he was here."

Her heart sank. "I don't know what he's gotten himself into," she said as her eyes welled with tears, "but whatever it is, I'll make good on it. If he owes someone money, just tell me, I'll pay them."

"I don't think it's as easy as that, Miss," he said, turning to face her again. "You can't turn back the pages of time. It's too late. The future has begun."

"What?" She scowled. "What kind of an answer is that?"

"I don't know where your brother is, Tyler." He placed his hands on her shoulders and spoke softly. "I see only what I'm supposed to see. Some things are closed off to me. You see, I have a smidgeon of clairsentience. Most of my psychic abilities are the result of learning to listen to what the ears cannot hear." He brushed away a strand of silky blonde hair that had fallen over the left side of her face. "But I think I know someone who may be able to help you."

The clanking of the cow bell announced another visitor to the shop. The old man held Tyler's face in his hands and patted her cheeks gently, then peered over her shoulder at his most recent visitor. His eyes brightened and a broad smile spread across his face. Tyler was curious to find out who could lift the old man's spirits so easily and turned to see a tall, dark haired man standing just inside the door. He was wearing blue jeans, a green and black plaid shirt with the sleeves rolled up, and hiking boots. He adjusted the strap of an overstuffed travel bag that hung over one broad shoulder, and his lips parted to expose a pearly white smile.

"Peter!" The old man walked around Tyler to greet him.

"Professor!" the man replied. He dropped the shoulder bag to the floor and embraced the old man.

Tyler scowled. "Professor? Ah, have I missed something here?" She watched the two men continue their celebration and at last they turned to face her after she had cleared her throat no less than a dozen times.

"I'm sorry, Missy, it's been quite some time since we've seen each other," the old man told her.

"I think I figured that out for myself," she said with a smile. "Perhaps I should be going. Give you two a chance to catch up."

"No, no, no," the fortune teller said. "Wait one moment please." He turned back to Peter, took him by the arm, and led him toward her. "Your timing, Peter–as usual–is perfect. Let me introduce you. Peter, this is Tyler Moore. Tyler, meet Peter Amado. He is the one I was just telling you about. If anyone can help you, he can."

Peter looked straight at her for the first time and his reaction was one of strange familiarity.

"I take it that you've met my brother, as well," she guessed from the way he was looking at her.

"Perhaps I have," he answered. He took her hand in his and bent to kiss the back of it gently. He lifted his head and looked up at her, and for a moment Tyler thought she was going to drown beneath the light blue ice of his eyes. *Who was this man that could stir such feelings within her at their first meeting?*

"Peter is gifted." The fortune teller interrupted their gaze.

"I'll just bet he is," she smiled.

"You can trust him," the old man told her.

She didn't need him to tell her that. It was something she just *knew*. She thought for a second that she was developing a bit of clairsentience as well, whatever that was, and then smiled at herself for thinking so. She looked away for fear he would see in her eyes what she was thinking, and fought the flush of red in her cheeks.

"More than I can say for you," she teased the old man. "So which is it? Professor or fortune teller?"

"A little of both, I guess," he laughed.

Peter pointed to the sign. "Yeah, what's this 'Visions of Valkner' crap?"

"And what's the matter with that?" The old man blew out a puff of air that lifted one side of his bushy mustache. He huffed over to the door and flipped a sign over with the "closed" facing out. "You think you have the monopoly on all the psychic mumble?"

Peter smiled broadly. "It sure is good to see you again, you cantankerous old goat." He stepped over to the old man and gave him a big squeeze, then turned to face Tyler, his face beaming with pride. "May I introduce to you–since he will most probably not introduce himself– the distinguished Professor James Valkner."

"Pleased, I'm sure," she bowed slightly and extended her hand. The old man shook it and gave her a wink.

"You can call me Jim. After all, Professor is a bit formal for a gal that's already had her hand in my britches. Wouldn't you say?" He winked at her again, and nodded at Peter who stood with a dropped jaw as the professor walked past him and into the back room.

"Ah ... yeah ... well," Peter stammered, "pay no attention to him," Peter told her. Then he leaned closer and whispered, "He sometimes gets moody like this."

"I heard that," the professor yelled from the back room. "Suppose you concentrate on helping the little lady instead of picking on a feeble old man."

"Feeble minded is more like it," Peter teased.

"I'm getting old, not deaf!" he barked.

Tyler couldn't help but chuckle. "Are you two always like this?"

"I'm sorry," he said, losing his smile. "All of this tomfoolery must seem so uncaring to you. Jim says you need some help. How might I serve you?" He looked at her with eyes so sincere she couldn't help but think he meant it.

"Find my brother," she answered, with a lump in her throat. It was all she could do to fight back the tears.

"I'll do my best," he promised. His voice was warm, and made her feel safe.

"That goes for me, too, young lady," the professor offered as he stepped through the beaded curtain at the back of the shop.

"That's right," Peter said, and smiled. "We're a team."

Tyler could see the love between them. Like a father and son. Somehow she felt she could trust them and she told them everything she knew. About the phone messages, her brother's habits, the cottage he'd rented for the remainder of the summer, and about the "vultures" that would be crawling all over him once they got wind of his discovery–whatever that was.

"Have you reported him missing?" the professor asked her.

"No," she sighed. "Given his past displays of irresponsibility, I thought I'd first investigate his whereabouts on my own. I've got to tell you, though, I'm seriously considering it now. It's not like him to make himself scarce for this long. I expected him to be hitting me up for some money by now." She couldn't help it. Her voice broke.

The professor put his arm around her shoulder and gave her a hug. "Now, now," he patted her arm, "not to worry, Missy, we'll help you. Won't we, Peter?" The professor nodded his head as if coaching an answer from Peter.

"Yes. Of course we will. I do think you should contact the authorities, though, and file a missing persons report. A little more help couldn't hurt," Peter advised.

"He's right," the professor agreed as he picked up the phone. "I'll get the sheriff on it right away. He's a friend of mine."

"In the meantime," Peter said, "I'd like to see the cottage."

"Of course. We can go there right now. I don't know what you'll find there, though. I just came from there and this is all I found." She held up the fortune teller's business card.

"I see. Well, another look wouldn't hurt." He turned to the professor. "Coming, old friend?"

The professor finished leaving his call back number, then hung up the phone and headed toward the door. "The store is closed," he pointed at the sign, "or haven't you noticed?"

"I guess you know there's no grass growing under his feet," Peter joked.

"Okay!" Tyler slapped her hands together, feeling relieved that she had some help and would soon find her brother. "Let's get this show on the road then. And guys," she added, "thanks." She watched them both smile at her, nodding their welcome, then turned and left the shop with them following her, leaving the clang of the cow bell behind them.

When they arrived at the cottage, Tyler opened the door and went in. The professor followed, but Peter lingered outside.

"Isn't he coming in?" she asked, peering over the old man's shoulder.

"He likes to prepare himself, mentally and spiritually, before inviting a vision."

Tyler's heart sank. *My God! She was with a couple of nuts!* She took a deep breath and tried to stay open minded. "A vision? Did you say he was going to invite a vision?" She prayed that she misunderstood.

"Yes. If he is successful, it could lead us to your brother."

Now that she understood. At this point, she'd try anything to find him. Another day would soon be over and she wanted nothing more than to lay her head on her pillow that night and know her brother was alright. If it meant putting up with a couple of eccentric nuts for an hour or so, so be it. She had handled crazier things for the magazine back in the early days. What bothered her most was knowing she was never going to live it down once Greg found out the route she'd taken in order to find him. But that didn't matter now. She just wanted to find him. To throw her arms around him, then punch his lights out.

She stood in line with the doorway, watching Peter. He was a fairly young man. She guessed about thirty-five. He seemed well educated. And the old man, well, he was a professor, for God's sake. She had no reason not to trust them. Not yet.

"You know, he asked to see the cottage and I don't even remember telling him about it. Nor you telling him about it. How did he...?"

"Oh, I gave up long ago trying to figure out how he knows what he knows. You'll drive yourself crazy trying to solve that one. I'm pretty sure you mentioned it, though," he said honestly.

"I'm sure I must have. I am just so stressed over this whole thing."

"I'm sure you are, dear."

"You've known each other for a long time?" she asked the professor, not once taking her eyes off of Peter.

"We worked together a few years ago," he said casually.

"A professor, huh?" She glanced at him, her eyes moved quickly over him from head to toe before turning her attention back to Peter. "I never would have guessed. So what do I call you? Swami, soothsayer, seer, or perhaps simply professor?"

"How about ... friend?" he suggested.

"Okay...friend." She watched Peter, who now knelt on one knee with his hands folded and placed to his lips. "I'll be honest with you, friend, I don't believe in all of this mumble jumble stuff. I never have. That's always been Greg's bag, not mine."

"Not to worry, Tyler. You don't have to believe in it for it to be so," he told her.

The statement cut her like a knife and broke her concentration on Peter. She looked at the professor and waited for an explanation. He didn't disappoint her.

"Peter has a gift that we call post-cognition. It's a displacement in time that allows him to visit places of which he has had no prior knowledge or memory. Sort of like watching a video that plays only in the mind's eye. A vision, if you will. It seems to occur spontaneously in everyday life and in dreams, but Peter–under supervision in countless parapsychology laboratory experiments–proved he could tap into the realm at will."

"So he is a true psychic in your professional opinion," she concluded.

He quickly shut his mouth and nodded. Peter was coming up the steps. Tyler took a deep breath and stood back, giving him lots of room should he feel the need to walk around. He appeared to her as a blind man. His eyes had a glazed over look to them. It reminded her of how her brother's eyes looked when he used to walk in his sleep when he was a kid. He scuffed across the floor and stopped directly in front of her. As his eyes closed, the loudest sound in the room was her breathing. She watched his eyes moving back and forth under his eyelids, much like the rapid eye movement that occurs while dreaming. *Could he see things beyond the realm of reality? Was she actually standing here watching this sideshow?* Before she could accept the answer, he opened his eyes, outstretched his arms, and lunged for her! Tyler stepped back in a panic and they both went tumbling to the floor, coming to rest with their faces only inches apart.

She looked into Peter's eyes and had the answer to her first question. His eyes were wild as if he had seen something horrific. She could tell he was trying to focus on her face, and for a moment thought he was going to scream, but then he pulled back and his eyes locked on to hers. He looked at her–through her–for what seemed an eternity, then he pulled his gaze from hers and stood up. He extended a hand to her and she wasn't surprised to find her hand shaking as she placed it in his. He pulled her to her feet, then turned without a word and walked to the cottage door. He stopped in the archway and stretched his arms overhead, resting them against the door casing. Tyler and the professor stood silently, watching him for the longest time, waiting for him to say something. When he finally turned to the professor to speak, her breath caught in her throat.

"You were right to call me," he said. Then he walked out of the cottage and Tyler watched him as he disappeared down the path.

CHAPTER 7–THE SEANCE

A day had passed since Peter's first visit to the cottage. This time he sat quietly on the top step with his back to the door, waiting for Tyler to wake up and let him in. Beside him were two large cups of Dunkin' Donut's coffees and a small bag containing a couple of glazed donuts. He hoped the offering would be accepted gracefully, paving the way for his explanation of his sudden departure the day before.

He looked past the pathway and out to sea. The early morning sun sparkled its rays across the water, teasing each and every wave to life. Its beauty filled him with hope and strength that he could overcome the evil that had lured him here. He outstretched his arms and took a deep breath of salty air, his elbows coming to rest on his knees as he exhaled, then he heard shuffling sounds inside the cottage. Tyler was awake. His stomach did a flip flop and at first he wanted to bolt from the steps, but he kept his cool. Soon the hinges began to squeak as Tyler opened the door.

"Well," she broke the silence, "are you just going to sit there, or are you going to come in and share a cup of that coffee with me?"

Peter dropped his head and smiled with relief, then he picked up his offering as he stood and faced her. She moved to the side of the doorway, allowing him to walk past her. It was a tight fit, and he heard her draw in her breath as he brushed against her. He sat the coffees and the donuts down on the dinette table, and she sat down opposite him. She said nothing as she removed the plastic lid from her cup of coffee and added three sugars. Peter was relieved. He had expected her to be giving him the third degree by now. He guessed she was as reluctant to hear the truth as he was to tell it. He watched her staring into the Styrofoam cup and knew her mind was flooded with worry for her brother. The silence grew between them, pounding like a drum in his ears. He had to speak or he was going to scream.

"Tyler, I want to tell you what hap..." She jumped to her feet so suddenly it made him gasp and sit upright in his chair.

"You know what? I think I'm going to change into a swim suit and catch a few rays." She marched over to her suitcase and pawed through it nervously, at last removing an aqua blue one piece suit.

"Tyler, we really have to talk about what I saw yesterday."

"Not now!" Her voice was sharp.

She hustled into the bathroom to change and

Peter could hear her elbows occasionally hit the walls of the narrow room as she frantically removed her clothing. There was a thud and the sound of a tin can rolling across the floor and then an outburst of profanity as he heard her kick the can again, only deliberately this time. The door opened and she walked out in a cloud of ashes with a few cigarette butts still stuck to the bottoms of her feet. She crossed the floor and opened the front door of the cottage with her head held high.

"I need some air," she said, and trotted down the steps, leaving the door open behind her. One might think she did so to invite him to follow her, but he didn't. He knew she needed some time alone.

Peter went to the bay window to watch her leave and saw the professor coming up the path. She passed him so quickly he nearly lost his balance trying to step aside so that she could pass by him. He stood there scratching his head, no doubt wondering what had gotten her in such an uproar first thing in the morning, then he turned and continued up the path. Peter heard him come up the steps and enter the cottage, but continued to watch Tyler, now down at the water's edge. She inched her way across mounds of rockweed to sit upon a huge boulder, its surface bleached white from the salt and sun.

"My! What happened here?" the professor asked. He fanned the cloud of ashes that still swirled in the air as he bent down to pick up a few of the scattered cigarette butts off the floor.

"Oh, Tyler had a little go-around with kick the can."

"Well, I'd say you're lucky it wasn't your butt she

kicked." He laughed, trying to make light of the situation. "Looks as if she didn't take it too well."

"She wouldn't listen to the first word I had to say. She's scared, that's all."

"And with good reason, I fear. Care to share it with an old friend?"

"Are you going to kick the can, too?" Peter finally pulled his gaze from Tyler and looked at the professor. They shared a smile, then Peter turned his eyes back to Tyler. "It's complicated, old pal."

Peter paused a long time before allowing himself to speak. He wished that not saying the words could somehow make it all go away, but in his gut he knew that wasn't to be so. Evil would not be denied. This he knew. He would have to acknowledge it even if it meant he would choke on his own words. The professor knew him well and was patient while he got his thoughts together.

"When I came up the steps, Jim, that's when I first felt it. *It.* I felt *it.*"

The professor looked at him. His eyes widened and he sucked in the drool that had begun to flow from the corner of his mouth. It made a slurping sound as he gulped some air and swallowed hard. Peter knew all too well what the professor was feeling. It was that fear and dread that made you forget how to breathe.

"The evil that I had just left in San Diego, the same evil that had found us in that apartment near Buffalo. Remember, Jim? Remember that?"

"Good God in heaven, Peter, how could I forget," he answered. His voice was a bit shaky and higher in pitch. He briskly rubbed his thick, gray mustache with the side of his forefinger on his right hand.

"Well," Peter went on, "it has found us again, only this time it wants to win. It's out for blood this time, Jim."

"Are you saying that all of these incidences are connected? That we're playing some kind of diabolical game here?"

"Oh, it's no game. Trust me. The rules have changed—profoundly."

The professor only looked at him. Afraid, no doubt, to ask what he meant by that. Peter saved him the trouble.

"There's been a murder," Peter blurted.

The professor began to pace. "Are you serious? Are you sure? Good God, Peter, you have to be sure before you go saying things like that."

"I'm sure."

The professor continued to walk back and forth. Peter couldn't. He couldn't move. He just wanted to look out the window and watch Tyler, and never think again about what he had seen when he had first entered the cottage the day before. But the more he looked out there at her, the more he knew he couldn't keep silent. He had to tell.

"Jim..." His voice was cutty and deep and echoed in the small room. The professor stopped in mid step and looked at him with big, round eyes, his lower lip dropping from under his bushy mustache. Peter knew by the look on his face that he would just as soon not hear the rest of what he was going to say. He could also see that he knew he was going to hear it anyway.

"When I stepped through that door yesterday, I was in another place and time. I was following a young man and his dog as they hiked along the shoreline, then suddenly I was standing in a room. At least I think it was a room. It may been a cave. It was dark and the air smelled and tasted like dirt."

As he told the professor about his vision, he was also remembering his reoccurring dream, the smell of the hole he and his brother Daniel had played in when they were kids, the taste of dirt in his mouth as he sat on the ground beside his car in the dessert, and the smell of a grave that lingered in his clothing after the vision he had in the house on Flintridge Drive. It was all coming together.

"The young man was there," Peter continued. "He was a few feet away from me, with his back turned to me. In my vision, I tried to walk closer to him, but I couldn't quite reach him. Then he saw something on a table in front of him that seemed to make him very happy. He walked to it, picked it up, and folded his arms over it, clutching it to his chest. Then he turned around and ..." Peter felt sick.

"And?"

"And I saw ... no...I *felt* a black mass pass through me and it killed him so fast he hardly knew what was happening."

"Dear God," the professor whispered. He closed his eyes and shook his head.

"I looked right into his eyes, Jim. I stood there and watched him get his throat ripped out." Peter clinched his jaws together.

"There was nothing you could do, Peter. You were

an observer, and that's all you were. You couldn't have done anything to help him. You know as well as I do that you can't change the past."

"But I'm going to change her future, aren't I, Professor," he said, looking out at Tyler sitting on the rock, safe from all the world. He sighed and rubbed the whisker stubble on his face with both hands. "How do I do that?"

"She doesn't know?"

Peter shook his head. "How do I tell her that when I came out of that trance yesterday and found myself face to face with her, I thought I was still looking into that young man's eyes?"

"Instead, you were looking at his twin." Now he understood.

"How do I tell her that I saw her brother murdered? Better yet, how do I tell her what I saw without her thinking I'm insane or that I derive some sort of perverted pleasure out of hurting her like this?"

The professor laid a hand on his shoulder. "Just tell her the truth, Peter. It's never failed you before."

"I know you're right. No sense in putting it off any longer. Besides, once that is done we can get started."

"Get started?" The professor scowled hard.

"Yeah. The end of a man's life is only the beginning." Peter looked at his old friend and saw dread in his eyes.

"The beginning? Of what?"

"Of sorrows. The beginning of sorrows."

The professor grunted as he walked across the floor to the door. "Why was I afraid you were going to say that?"

Peter ignored his remark and turned to look out of the window again. "When you come back, bring the materials we'll need to make contact."

"Ah, there it is," the old man grumbled as he left the cottage. "No sleep for a weary old man tonight."

Peter laughed to himself. He loved the old man, even if he was a complainer. He had a knack of keeping Peter's feet on the ground. The old man stood for stability, and Peter needed that in his life. And the old fellow was right, he needed to tell Tyler the truth. He looked at her sitting on the rock and knew there was no sense in delaying it any longer. He had to talk to her now, and try to get her to understand.

The tide was exceptionally low and it was a long walk to where Tyler sat on the rock. The air was pungent with salt and smelled of fish and raw clams. Peter made his way over the rocks that were slick with a light green slime and covered with long strands of dark green, bulbous seaweed. He was proud of himself to have made it within inches of the rock without incident, when suddenly his feet flew out from under him and his butt made contact with the mucky bottom of the cove.

"Need some help?" Tyler had turned around on the rock and was facing him with a hand outstretched. She immediately closed her mouth and held her lips tightly together, no doubt trying to conceal her laughter.

"No," he replied sarcastically, "I think I'll just lay here and wait until the tide comes in and washes me ashore."

"Ho. Ho." She grabbed his hand and pulled him up. She was fairly strong. Once on his feet, he leaped upon the rock, but winced a little as he sat down beside her.

"About yesterday, Tyler," he said softly, "I'd like to explain what happened."

"I'm sorry I walked out on you earlier. I just couldn't bring myself to listen. You know the "no news is good news" mentality. Jim must have thought I was so rude. I should apologize to him."

"Nah, don't worry about him. He's a tough old bird. Besides, he's very forgiving." He smiled at her and winked.

"Well, I've had some time to think, and I know running away isn't the answer. So, if you have something to tell me about my brother, Mr. Amado, then I need to hear it."

"Even if it's not good?"

"Especially."

Peter took a deep breath and looked out to sea, trying to find the right words to tell her what he had seen. There were no right words. No easy way to say it. Then—

"Is he alive?" Her voice quivered. She, too, was looking out at sea.

"I think not." The words hurt his throat as he said them. Tyler turned to him, sobbing on his chest. The tears felt hot as they soaked through his shirt. He wrapped his left arm around her and tried to hold her close, but she pulled away and hit his chest three times with her fist. He let her. He had expected this. She stopped and sobbed against him again.

"Tyler, I know you're angry. You want me to be wrong, and God knows I want to be," he said gently, "but that doesn't change what I saw."

She pulled back from him and looked into his eyes. "What you 'saw'? Do you hear yourself?" Her voice got louder and its tone said she thought he was nuts, then it turned angry. She jumped down off the rock and Peter slid off in an effort to grab her arm to slow her down. Somehow he knew there would be no stopping her. "Well, you hear me! You are wrong! You're just like all the others that Greg spent hours chasing after. You're all out for a buck. I just haven't figured you and the old man out yet, what your scam is, but I will," she snapped. "And when I do, there'll be hell to pay, Peter Amado. Hell to pay!" She stomped off.

Peter stood beside the rock, watching her run from the truth. He yelled, "Do you want proof?"

She stopped.

He spoke easier this time. His voice carried on the wind. "I can give you that. There is a way."

She spun around and looked across the mounds of seaweed between them. "How?" she yelled against the wind.

"A séance."

"A séance? You're bloody nuts! Do you know that? A séance is used to speak with the dead, and my brother is not dead!" She screamed at him.

"I pray you're right, Tyler, but you must let me try. If I'm wrong, I'm wrong and all is right with the world, but God help me if I'm right, then someone must pay."

Tyler straightened and took a deep breath. She

paused for a couple of minutes, and he waited.

"Okay. Okay, Peter, I'll go along with it. But I warn you, it'll not be easy to convince me with parlor tricks."

Peter walked up to where she stood. His shirt, where her searing tears had fallen, was now cold against his skin. He wanted so badly to pull her to him and absorb her warmth, but he kept his distance. He nodded and walked past her and back to the cottage. *Let her be angry. It will keep her strong.* As he entered the cottage he could hear her coming up the path behind him. It was a good sign.

While waiting for the professor to return, their conversation was nothing more than meaningless chatter that served only to burn minutes off the clock. A chill was in the air, and Peter wasn't sure if there had actually been a change in the season, or if it was only a preliminary glimpse of what was to come that evening. He paced a path from the stove to the open door, wringing his hands. Once in a while he blew out a breath of air, like a kettle venting steam, trying to relieve the stress of waiting. Finally, he looked out to see the professor coming up the pathway.

"Don't just stand there gawking at me," the professor yelled. "Give me some help here!" He was struggling with a suitcase in one hand, a small round table in the other, and a board game tucked under his right arm.

Peter dashed out the door and relieved the old man of his burden. "Gosh, I'm sorry, Jim. I wasn't thinking when I asked you to bring all of this stuff." Peter took the items off his hands, but hesitated a little when he slipped the board game out from under the professor's arm. It was a Ouija board.

"What's the matter, Peter?" the professor said gruffly. "What did you think we were going to play? Monopoly?"

"You know how I feel about these things, Jim. I just wish there was another way."

The professor shook a stiff, yet unsteady finger at him. "Sometimes you have to fight fire with fire, my boy."

"Well, it's not how I operate," he fumed.

"True. But it *is* how I operate," he growled and snatched the board away from Peter. "Are we going to stand out here all night and argue philosophy or help that little lady in there find out what happened to her brother?"

Peter stepped aside and let him pass. The professor reminded him of Deke. When he was nervous, he was a bear to be around, too. Although he was sure the professor had more on his mind than what they were about to do in the cottage. He felt sorry now that he had reminded him of days gone by–as if he wouldn't have thought of it anyway. Fact was, he knew neither of them would ever stop thinking about what had happened in that little apartment outside of Buffalo. Not ever.

Peter stepped into the cottage and placed the items in the center of the room. The professor set up the table and removed a note pad and pen from the small suitcase, then he went into the kitchen and poured himself some water. Peter didn't wonder why. His mouth had gone dry, too.

Tyler sat on the loveseat, taking it all in. She was trying to look smug, like she wasn't going to fall for any of their nonsense, but Peter could see through her facade. She was afraid.

"Any questions before we get started?" Peter asked her.

"Oh, only about a few thousand," she said nervously.

"Not to worry." He smiled at her. "We'll guide you through this."

"Peter," the professor called from the kitchen. "May I speak with you for a moment?"

"Excuse me," he said to Tyler, then walked over to where the professor stood. "Just a word of warning, Peter," he half whispered. "You are a channeler. You must make sure that *only* Gregory Moore visits here tonight."

He didn't say who else he thought might drop by, but Peter knew who he meant. "Believe me, my old friend, if another visits here tonight, it'll not be by my invitation."

The professor nodded and looked relieved, then he peered over Peter's shoulder. Peter knew what he was looking at, he could feel Tyler standing behind him, straining to hear every word. He swung around to face her.

"Tyler, are you ready to begin?"

"Who might be joining us tonight?" It was plain to see, she wasn't going to let him change the subject so easily.

"No one," Peter insisted. "Shall we get started?" He rubbed his hands together, trying to warm them, as he went to the small round table. "If all of this bothers you,

you can wait outside."

"And take your word for what happens?" She shook her head. "I don't think so. I'll not be driven out by your parlor games. I'll stay, if for nothing else than to prove to you that you're wrong." She sat back down on the loveseat and crossed her arms.

The professor cleared his throat when he came to the table as if he was interrupting quarreling lovers. He opened the Ouija board on top of the small round table and placed the tear shaped oracle on top of it. He lit two candles and placed one on each side of the board so that all the letters would be illuminated.

"Tyler and I can share the loveseat. If you'll pull over one of those dinette chairs for yourself, Peter, we can get started." He picked up the note pad and pen and passed it to Tyler. "Perhaps you would consider helping us by taking notes."

"Notes?" She hesitantly took the pad and pen.

"Peter, you'll ask the questions, I'll say aloud the letters, and Tyler, you'll write them down. Agreed?"

Peter and Tyler nodded in agreement. The professor then removed from the suitcase a small voice activated tape recorder and placed it on the sideboard in the kitchen.

"These things most often malfunction during these types of sessions," he mumbled, "but we'll give it a try anyway." He took his place in front of the loveseat, still standing, and looked at each of them. "All set are we?" Peter looked only at Tyler and she looked only at him.

"Are you sure you're alright with this?" Peter asked her.

"Let's get it over with," she replied. Then she flipped back the front cover on the notepad and took the pen in her hand as she sat on one end of the loveseat, ready for dictation. The professor smiled at her as he sat down next to her.

"Then let's begin," Peter said, and walked to the door and turned off the lights. Their shadows flickered on the walls like an old silent movie as Peter began to pray.

"Dear God in heaven, protect your faithful servants that no evil shall enter in. Amen."

"Amen." Tyler and the professor both said together.

Peter and the professor placed the tips of their fingers on the oracle and at once it began to move around on the board. The movement was slow and jerky at first, then it increased in speed and glided smoothly in large circles. Tyler sat watching intently. Peter surmised she was trying to decide which one of them was pushing the oracle around on the board.

"We must all clear our minds and think only of Gregory. We want only to speak with Gregory," the professor insisted. Peter nodded.

"Gregory, can you hear us?" Peter asked.

The oracle moved wildly around the board and came to rest over a word. The professor looked through the plastic porthole on the oracle and read aloud the word.

YES

Tyler's mouth dropped open. It was clear she

didn't believe and even more clear that she was appalled that they would tease her about such a thing. Peter knew there was nothing he could do to convince her. She would have to learn the truth for herself. He only hoped that she could handle it.

The oracle began to move again, only more erratic. Peter thought it was going to fly right out from under their fingertips as he and the professor struggled to keep their hands on its tear-shaped form. The shutters on the bay windows began to rattle violently and a deep rumble came from the bowels of the house. It reminded Peter of the sound he had heard once during a California earthquake. It had woke him from his sleep and had moved him and his bed across the room. He looked again at Tyler. Where first there was doubt, now there was fear. The vibration they were experiencing now was not an earthly occurrence. Peter was at least sure of that. This vibration was an awakening of evil, and it shook him down to the absolute core of his being. The tin basin danced wildly in the sink. Its rim bounced above the edges of the sideboard. Tyler watched it with wide eyes, only glancing periodically at the shaking, wooden shutters, then right back to the clattering pan.

"What the heck is ..." Tyler scowled.

"Sh!" The professor demanded quiet and continued to watch Peter intently.

Though the shutters remained closed, a cool breeze swirled around the room, lifting the pages on the notepad that Tyler had thrown down on the loveseat. She pulled her feet up under her and sat on her knees. Backing as far away from the notepad as the loveseat would allow, she looked as if she didn't think things could get any wilder. Then Peter felt–*the tug.*

"Focus, Peter," the professor told him. He seemed to be ignoring the wind and noise. "You know why you have been called."

Peter tried to maintain contact with the spirit that had identified itself as Gregory, but something was pulling him to a place he didn't want to go. Something that wanted control. He fought to concentrate on their purpose, but his mind was being filled with images of destruction and mayhem. Then suddenly, the windows stopped shaking and an eerie stillness fell upon the cottage. There was a sound that reminded Peter of the north wind that had howled around the side of the house he'd lived in when he was a kid, then he realized the sound was actually the air being sucked out of the cottage.

"What's happening? I can't breathe." Tyler wheezed, clutching her throat.

"Dear God, help us," Peter prayed. "Cover us with your almighty blood. The blood that was shed for us. We plead, Lord Jesus, to be covered with the precious blood of the Lamb."

In mid prayer, the room's air pressure returned to normal, and they sat quietly for a few moments, and took several deep breaths. Tyler didn't say anything. Peter could see she was stunned by what had just happened, and was trying to explain it all away in her own mind. He could have told her, it wasn't going to happen that easily.

Again Peter demanded to speak with Gregory Moore. He could see Tyler bite her tongue at the mention of his name. He thought she would have fled by now, but she stayed. He suspected she was determined–even after the display the spirit world had just put on for them–to prove them wrong. She couldn't and wouldn't believe her brother was dead.

An agonizing moan mingled with the sound of the waves breaking against the rocky shoreline as Peter called upon Gregory Moore. The oracle moved again, only this time it moved smoothly and in full circles around the board. "Are you the spirit of Gregory Moore?" Peter asked.

The oracle came to rest and the professor read the message aloud.

YES

Tyler had been sitting with her legs doubled underneath her, trying to watch every corner of the room, but when this answer came she managed to overcome her fright and pick up the notepad to record the letters.

"We demand proof of your identity. If you are Gregory Moore, there is one among us who knows you well. Give her a sign that only she will recognize, then we will know the truth."

YES THE TRUTH

They sat silently, waiting for something to happen, and when it did it wasn't at all what they had expected. No materialization, no floating orbs of light, nor possession. It began as a faint odor, then increased to a stench that had Peter and the professor gagging on the wicked scent. Peter looked at Tyler. She seemed not to mind the smell at all. She sat there quietly, looking at the board, a tear rolling down her cheek.

"Tyler?" Peter spoke to her.

She tilted her head back slightly and slowly lifted

her eyes to look at him. "It's Greg. It's him," she cried.

Peter wanted to hold her, but he couldn't remove his fingers from the oracle. It held him there like a vice, threatening to never let him go. The professor nodded his head for Peter to go on with the questions. There was still so much more they needed to know.

"Have you come to me before?" Peter asked the spirit.

YES

Tyler again bit her tongue and glared at Peter. Peter turned his eyes away from her and focused on the board. He knew what the answer to his next question was going to be, but he needed to ask it anyway.

"Was your death a natural death, Gregory?"

An angry, disembodied audible voice yelled, *"NO!"*

Tyler and the professor nearly jumped out of their skins at the sudden vocal blast from the spirit realm, but Peter couldn't move. The sound of the spirit's voice had sent him to a place where they could not visit. A place Peter wished he could run away from. Yet, he knew that wasn't possible, for it was a place within his own mind.

There he could see black forms moving in the darkness. They circled him, closing in on him each time they went around, until they were close enough that he could make out that they were wearing black, hooded robes. He tried to count them. There were twelve. No, there were thirteen. Thirteen of them. He watched them as one by one the robed figures merged one with the other, until there were only two forms remaining.

Suddenly, the vision ended and Peter was jolted back to reality as the oracle began to move again under his fingertips. The professor read off the letters and waited for Tyler to separate them into words and read them aloud.

YOU MUST STOP THEM

"Who must we stop?" Peter asked, still somewhat dazed from his recent vision.

FLED SALEM

"My brother was in Salem," Tyler whispered.

"Sh!" the professor scolded.

"Who fled Salem? A coven?" Peter's questions drew another strange look from Tyler.

YES

"When?"

The oracle moved around the board restlessly before finally answering.

1692

"What's that got to do with the here and now? Or Gregory's death?" The professor forgot himself and blurted out.

"Sh!" Tyler hushed him. Peter looked up at her and they shared a brief smile.

The oracle continued to move from letter to letter.

THEY LIVE

"The coven still exists?" This time Peter got a strange look from the professor, too.

NO TWO REMAIN

All of a sudden, as electricity leaving a wire, the power that had moved the oracle was gone. They sat silently, looking at one another, trying to digest what had just happened. Finally, Peter got up and turned on the light, then walked back to the table and blew out the candles. Tyler sat, motionless, and she looked so sad. Peter reached down and removed the notepad from her hands and they went limp and fell in her lap. She looked at him with blank eyes.

"Are you okay?" Peter asked her.

"It was the same," she said lifelessly.

"What was the same?" Peter asked.

"It had to be him. There was no way you could have known." She was in shock.

"What's that, dear?" the professor asked her gently.

She looked at them both, first one then the other, with eyes now filled with pain and sadness. It was clear she was having a hard time accepting what had happened and the revelation of its meaning.

"Greg and I weren't always close." She struggled with the words. "I guess it had to do with our being twins and always searching for our own identity. He just wanted to be included in everything I did with my friends, and I was bent on doing everything I could to exclude him. So my friends and I started a secret club. A girl's club." Now she smiled as she thought back. "Oh, he hated me for that. He swore he'd get even. Well, he did alright. He made a stink bomb with a chemistry set he'd gotten the previous Christmas and he set it off in my room. I couldn't sleep in my room for weeks and everything I owned reeked of rotten eggs. It was a month before the girls in the club would let me back in their meetings. I thought he'd never stop laughing over that one." She let out a laugh as she finished the story, then became solemn again. "You smelled it, too. It was awful, wasn't it?"

"Yeah, Tyler. It was an awful smell," Peter replied. His voice broke, as did his heart for her as he sat on the loveseat and placed his arms around her. He never noticed when the professor left the cottage. All he was aware of was the weight of Tyler's head on his shoulder and the burden he felt for not being able to relieve her pain. They sat silently with the light still burning brightly in the cottage and waited for sleep to take them.

Dawn came with the cackle of sea gulls. Peter awoke, thinking a night dragger must have brought its catch in to the pier. Tyler was still asleep, and Peter wiggled his right arm out from under her. She stirred briefly, keeping her eyes shut tight, then laid down on the loveseat and pulled her knees closer to her mid-section. Peter covered her gently with a small blanket that had found its way into his shoulder bag before leaving the airplane. She snuggled down beneath it and embraced blissful sleep.

Peter, on the other hand, got little if any rest. When the first crack of sunshine filtered through the wooden slats of the shutters covering the bay window, it was like a ray of hope. A sign that another day was to go on. Another battle was yet to be won. He shook his head, not wanting to think of that just yet. He looked instead at Tyler. She looked so peaceful. Sleep had wiped the tension from her face, and he wished she could stay like that, but he knew when she awoke she'd have the truth to face again, and it was going to be painful. He wanted to be there for her, to hold her and tell her everything was going to be alright, but he didn't know if he could do that. Not truthfully. He wasn't sure about what they were facing, but felt it was bigger and more powerful than any of them could imagine.

The seasons in the northeast change so rapidly, and this morning was a true testament of it. There was quite a chill in the morning air, and Peter decided he'd get some wood for the stove. He hadn't been able to get his hands warm since before the séance. He thought he remembered seeing bundles of firewood for sale at the village store. He'd possibly be able to buy some instant coffee there, too. He was sure Tyler would enjoy a hot cup when she woke up.

He opened the door of the cottage quickly to avoid the drawn out squeal of the door hinges and went outside. The sun was just peeking over an island about a mile from the mainland. There wasn't even the slightest breeze, and the water was like glass. He inhaled deeply, and was drunk with the sights, sounds, and smells of the seaside village. As he walked out the long pathway to the pier he saw the sea gulls that had lured him from sleep. They covered the tin roof of the wharf, singing praises to the morning sun. As he got closer to the village store he saw the closed sign still in the window and not a stick of wood left outside, so he crossed the street to the professor's house. He followed a walkway around the left side of the building and through a window he could see the professor sitting at the kitchen table sipping a cup of hot tea. He looked up and saw Peter and motioned for him to come in.

"Morning, Jim."

"Same to you, my friend. Tyler's not with you?" He peered behind Peter.

"She's still asleep. I didn't have the heart to wake

her."

"Poor kid. I wish there was something we could do for her," he said. "It's hard enough to lose a sibling, but a twin ..." He shook his head as he wound the string from his tea bag around the handle of his mug. "Want a cup?"

"Actually, I thought I might be able to borrow a coffee pot and some grounds. The store's not open yet."

"Sure. You know I'm a tea drinker, but I always keep some coffee on hand to offer my clients." He got up and went to the cupboard. "As a matter of fact, I think I still have an old aluminum campfire coffee pot here somewhere." He opened a cupboard under the sink and rattled a few pans before pulling it out. "Yeah, here it is," he said, and placed it in front of Peter on the table. He grabbed a one pound can of Maxwell House coffee and passed it to Peter. "Have you got any wood at the cottage?"

"Nope. I was hoping to get some of that at the store, too"

"No need. I've got plenty stored in the shed for the winter. When you leave, take one of those baskets by the door and take however much you need."

"Thanks, Jim. The cottage sits back under the trees and it's a little nippy this morning." He got up to leave. "I'd better get back before Tyler wakes up. I don't know how she'd feel about being there alone after last night. I can't say that I'd blame her if she never wanted to see that cottage again."

"That was nerve wracking for me, too. I'm getting too old for this stuff, Pete."

"Nah," Peter waved him off, "you're just getting

started." Peter flashed him a smile and winked.

The professor saw him to the door, pointing out the basket and the woodshed. "I'll stroll on over to the cottage sometime before noontime. Maybe we can all take a ride into Bath and grab some lunch."

Peter nodded, thinking only of Tyler and getting her out of the cottage for a while. He loaded everything he needed into the basket and headed toward the seaside path. When he got back to the cottage he found Tyler still asleep, and breathed a sigh of relief. Quietly he went to the stove and placed the basket next to it. In the kitchen cupboard he found the poker for removing the top burner lid, and ripped off a few pieces of the paper grocery bag that sat on the counter to use to set the kindling afire. Before long, the wood was ablaze, snapping and crackling inside the stove, warming the entire cottage within half an hour. The coffee pot began to perk, spitting the darkening brew into its clear glass bubble on top of the lid. Peter moved it to the back of the stove so it wouldn't burn. Its aroma filled the room and teased Tyler into wakefulness.

"Morning," Peter said, passing her a cup of freshly brewed coffee.

She sat up on the loveseat with the small blanket still wrapped around her shoulders and took the cup in both hands. Her eyes were a little puffy from sleeping too long or from crying in her sleep, he couldn't tell which, but she was still beautiful. Not even anguish could take that from her.

"What time is it?" she asked. Her voice was a raspy whisper.

"Eight thirty."

"My goodness! Why didn't you wake me?" She started to get up, but Peter reached out and patted her arm, and she settled back down. "I've got to call the magazine."

"There will be time for that. Just drink your coffee. Besides, there isn't any cell phone service in this area. You'll have to use Jim's phone."

"I've got to admit, it's the best tasting cup of coffee that I've ever had." She looked at the old campfire coffee pot. "What were you, a boy scout?"

"Something like that." He smiled and sipped from the cup he cradled in his hands.

She got up and walked to the stove with the blanket still draped around her shoulders and held out a hand to absorb the heat. "I'm not really sure of what happened here last night," she said with her back to him. "Maybe I dreamt the whole thing."

"I tell myself that all the time," he said. "I wish it were true."

"Then it did happen. God, Peter, this is insane. Things like this don't happen."

"Believe me, they do."

"Not to me, they don't. I'm the logical one. The level headed one. The debunker."

"So was I–once."

"We have no *real* proof that Gregory is ..." She couldn't finish the sentence.

Peter walked up behind her and placed his hands on her shoulders. He could smell the perfume in her hair. It was sweet. As sweet as her voice.

"I promise you, Tyler, we'll find him. We're not going to give up until we do."

She turned around and faced him, and looked at him for some time, as if trying to figure him out. "Why do I feel so connected to you? We just met. Why do I feel that I can trust you completely?"

"I think it's because of my irresistible charm," he joked. "All the boy scouts have it." She didn't comment, but her eyes sparkled when she smiled at him.

They drank another cup of coffee while sitting on the front steps of the cottage. The sun had warmed the day nicely, and they were content to sit without talking. They watched the fishing boats out in the bay as the lobster fishermen pulled up their traps. It was business as usual for them. They had no idea what evil lurked in their village.

Before long, the professor came up the path and asked if they were ready for lunch. They wasted no time leaving the cottage and right after Tyler called the magazine they left for town. Within twenty minutes after that, they were parked on Front Street in Bath near a small deli. A sign in the window advertised the deli's famous lobster rolls and crabmeat salad–something Peter hadn't had the luxury of enjoying in California.

When they walked in, a waitress greeted them from across the room and told them to have a seat wherever they pleased and she'd be with them in a moment. They chose a booth on the far side of the room. Tyler sat on one side with the professor and Peter slid across the seat opposite Tyler. The waitress came right over and took their orders. Peter and Tyler ordered the lobster roll with a side of New England clam chowder.

The professor ordered a pastrami with mustard on rye. The service was fast and they finished eating within thirty minutes or so. The waitress came around with the coffee pot and gave them all refills. She looked around at all the empty tables and told them to take their time. It was a slow business day. The professor insisted on paying for their lunch and gave the waitress at least a 25 percent tip. She left them to their coffee with a smile on her face that not even the short tempered cook behind the counter could erase. That left them to talk about the only thing that was on any of their minds— the previous night's ordeal.

"I think we need to try it again. Tonight," Peter suggested.

"So do I," the professor seconded.

Tyler said nothing. She didn't have to. The look on her face spoke volumes. She had gone pale, except for a round circle of deep red on each cheek. She wiped her mouth nervously with her napkin as her eyes darted back and forth from Peter to the professor. Peter could tell she didn't like this one little bit. He watched her as she watched the professor's shaky hands remove from his pocket three folded sheets of paper from the notebook she had recorded the messages on during the séance, then listened while he began to read.

"The spirit's words said, 'You must stop them.' When asked, 'Who?' the spirit revealed a coven that existed in the year 1692 and suggested that two members of that coven still exist."

"That's preposterous!" Tyler blurted.

"Maybe not," Peter told her.

"Explain," the professor urged.

"Yeah," Tyler scoffed, "I'd like to hear how you explain that one, too."

"I don't know if I can. I only know that during the séance I had a vision of what I now believe was a coven. The black robed figures in my vision merged one with another until only two remained. I could feel the power emanating from the two figures. It was stronger than anything I had ever felt before. It was as if the two had absorbed the life-force of the other coven members."

The professor sat thoughtfully, combing the side of his mustache with his thumb and forefinger. Peter knew the old man well. This meant he had a theory.

"Okay, let's hear it, Jim," Peter prodded.

"Hear what?" Tyler was still in the dark.

The professor sighed and shook his head. "I don't know that I'm right. God help us if I am."

"Spill it, Jim. We're grownups," Peter said.

"There is a ritual, buried deep in literature, that suggests a true believer can inherit the powers of another–their 'life-force' if you will–through a diabolic ceremony," the professor tried to explain.

"The merging that I witnessed," Peter concluded.

The professor nodded. "It would explain your vision and why the spirit said two remain."

Tyler pushed back from the table and spoke loudly, drawing the unwanted attention from a few of the diners that remained in the deli. "Get serious! That's impossible," she blurted. She was quickly hushed by the professor and Peter. She then continued with a whisper. "That would make them over three hundred years old.

Utterly ridiculous." She tried to dismiss the idea.

"As ridiculous as a talking dead man, don't you think?" Peter reminded her. Her face flushed.

"We're getting nowhere with this," the professor interrupted. "We need more answers. We need to know exactly what we're up against here. Another séance is the only way."

"I agree," Peter said, and looked at Tyler for her approval. He was aware of her hesitation as he watched her rub her hands together as if trying to warm them. He knew only too well what that feeling was like. Finally she let out a long sigh and nodded her head.

"Then we are all in agreement, we'll try again tonight," the professor said.

"Tonight," Tyler confirmed.

With that said, they got up from the table and left the deli. It was a quiet ride back to Sebasco. Peter surmised they each had their own reservations about the séance. None of them could be sure that the spirit believed to be Gregory Moore could help them. Tyler seemed convinced that it was Gregory that they had contacted. Peter wasn't completely sold on it. He had been lied to before.

The professor pulled into his driveway and turned off the engine, inviting them into his house for tea. Tyler gracefully declined, saying she was going to go back to the cottage and lay down for a while. Peter was much too keyed up for that. He said he was going to change into a pair of shorts and take a dip in the cove nearby. The professor wished them a pleasant afternoon and said he would see them that evening for the séance.

In no time they were back at the cottage and Peter thought he saw Tyler's eyes close before she had even laid down on the loveseat. He changed into his shorts and told her he'd be back before dark. She grunted a reply and kept her eyes tightly closed. Peter shut the door quietly behind him and started his walk down to the cove. The warm afternoon sun had devoured his memory of the morning's chill, and he was looking forward to a refreshing swim.

The tide was at ebb so he kicked off his sandals and left them at the head of the cove on a mound of rockweed. Carefully he made his way across a bed of broken seashells, welcoming the muddy clam flats as he neared the water. He wasn't prepared for the icy Atlantic and at first it took his breath away when he stepped into it, but he braved the sting of the cold and continued to walk out deeper into the blue-green water until he was about waist deep. His legs were already going numb from the cold and soon he was able to plunge beneath the surface. He could feel the water's pressure as it surrounded him and muffled the sounds from above. The air in his lungs began to expand and he exhaled a cloud of bubbles as he ascended to the surface. He swam out to a marker buoy just beyond the mouth of the cove, and there he floated on his back letting the sun's rays warm his face.

He tried not to think of anything but peaceful thoughts, but then images of his vision of Gregory flashed before his eyes and reminded him that evil was never far away. Suddenly, being so far from shore made him nervous. The water beneath him turned black and he felt if he didn't swim for shore now, the darkness would pull him in. He struggled to keep himself from slipping into its evil, and with long, powerful strokes he swam back toward shore. The moment his fingertips touched the bottom, he stood and waded to dry land. He laid down on a smooth ledge, breathing heavily. He wasn't sure if it was the adrenaline rush or pure embarrassment that was warming him from the inside out. He laughed at himself and shook his head as he tried to relax against the flat rock. The surface radiated warmth and the sun and a gentle breeze began to dry him. The warmth induced a heaviness that slowly lured him into sleep, only to awaken in a dream.

In this world, between reality and hope, he was standing in front of a church with bright red doors. The doors slowly opened, but there was no one to be seen. Then he heard a voice, soft and low, speak to him. The voice was comforting and made him feel safe. It said, "Come, Peter. Come in and I will give you peace." Peter wanted to see to whom the voice belonged and walked through the archway, but everything began to fade to white.

He awoke. The sun was just going down behind the seafood freezer plant. He had been napping for quite some time. The tide was nearly all the way up into the head of the cove and his sandals were afloat at the water's edge. He scooped them up and slipped them on his feet and headed back to the cottage. He knew the professor would be arriving soon for the séance, and Tyler would be getting nervous once the sun set, so he hurried up the path and went into the cottage.

"Oh there you are," Tyler shouted from the kitchen. "I was beginning to think I was going to have to eat this all by myself." She came from the kitchen holding a salad bowl with both hands and set it down on the table. She had two places set, each holding a steak and a baked potato.

"Smells great! Not only are you easy on the eyes, but you're a great cook, too."

"Ha. Ha."

"How did you ever come up with all of this?"

"I paid Jim a visit, borrowed a few things, got directions to a decent market, and voila! Dinner for two."

"Well, I'm impressed," Peter said, watching her light a candle she had placed in the center of the table. "And hungry," he added. "Let me wash up and change my clothes real quick." He dashed into the rest room.

"Make it fast. This won't stay hot much longer," she yelled at him. He didn't need her to tell him twice.

The meal was delicious. Tyler had cooked the steak just the way he liked it—medium rare. He wolfed it down and thought she would think him unmannerly, but he could see by the twinkle in her eyes that she was pleased that he liked it so much. After dinner they talked about everything except what was going to happen that evening. Tyler told him all about her career in the magazine business. How she had worked her way up to being the pictorial layout editor for one of the fastest growing fashion magazines on the market. In turn, he told her all about his affiliation with Deke and the countless investigations of haunted houses and demented crackpots. He even managed to get a laugh or two out of her, and that really pleased him. She was beautiful, especially when she laughed.

Then the conversation changed to the days when he and the professor worked together in Buffalo. It made him remember the case he wanted to forget, and he was sure she was baffled when he quickly changed the subject. He didn't want to go into that part of his life. Not tonight. When she began to question him about it, he was relieved to hear the sound of the professor coming up the cottage steps, and jumped up from his chair to greet him.

"Please, come in, Jim," Peter said to him. Tyler got up and began clearing the table. Peter opened the door for the professor then went back to the table and helped her until it was wiped clean.

"I hope I'm not too early," the professor spoke loudly so that they could hear him from the living room.

"Not at all, Jim. We had just finished eating. You have perfect timing," Peter assured him. "Thanks for helping Tyler pull this together. I haven't had a home cooked meal for some time, and it was delicious."

"Don't let him pull your leg, Professor, it was just a simple meal."

"Simple for a gourmet cook perhaps, but for me it was a slice of Heaven."

"Oh, you..." She ribbed him and came out of the kitchen with a smile on her face. "Where's the Ouija board? I'll set it up," she said, looking around for it, trying so hard to be brave.

"Oh, we won't be using it tonight," the professor informed her.

"Oh. Has there been a change of plans?" she asked. She looked first at Peter then the professor.

"No," Peter told her. "We won't need it. Contact has already been made."

"He's right," the professor said. "Peter will serve as the board tonight. The spirit will speak through him."

Peter could see that Tyler was a bit upset by the

turn of events. She thought she had a handle on what was going to happen only to find out the game plan had changed. She took it well, though, and stayed calm.

"Do I take notes like I did last night?"

"Actually, we'd like your help at the table tonight, if you don't mind," the professor answered her.

"To do what?" It was clear she was more than just a little nervous.

"Relax, Tyler. Everything will be alright," Peter assured her. "You only have to sit here and hold our hands. We'll do the rest."

"Sounds easy," she said. Her eyes darted from one to the other and she swallowed hard. "Then why am I shaking in my boots?"

"It'll be alright. I promise," Peter told her.

"Then let's get it over with, shall we," she said as she sat down on the loveseat in front of the small, round folding table.

The professor brought the candle from the dinner table and placed it in the center of the round table, and Peter turned off the lights and took his seat. They bowed their heads as Peter said a prayer, asking for protection and divine guidance, then the séance began. He sat with his eyes closed, yet it seemed he could see the others clearly.

"Let us join hands, and no matter what happens, don't break the circle," the professor warned. "We must clear our minds and think only of Gregory. We want only to speak with Gregory. Can you hear us, Gregory? Will you come to us?"

They sat quietly. Waiting.

"We have questions that only you can answer, Gregory. Come and help us. Help us to find you so that we may lead you to rest," the professor continued to plead with the spirit.

Peter sensed a presence in the room, but it wasn't Gregory Moore. It was evil. Suddenly he felt as if the air was being squeezed out of him, and he could see the others were experiencing the same feeling.

The professor struggled to speak. "Who are you?"

Immediately, in the far corner of the room a figure appeared. Tyler gasped as she looked at the form in a black hooded robe. Peter gripped her hand, urging her to be still. The figure's face was hidden by the hood, but all were sure it was not Gregory Moore. Above the black robed figure the Beast appeared. Unlike the robed figure, its body was transparent. It tilted back its horned head and roared, causing the entire cottage to shake. Then it vanished.

Tears were now streaming down Tyler's cheeks, and Peter thought she was going to go screaming out of the cottage, but instead she gripped his hand tighter, her nails digging into his palm. He squeezed her hand trying to reassure her that everything was going to be alright, and prayed to God that he would be able to make good on the promise.

The robed figure lifted its head and glided across the floor toward them. It had the face of an old woman and its eyes were two glowing orbs of fire. It opened its mouth and from it came the wailing of all the tormented souls of hell. Peter began to pray at once, raising his voice to be heard above the screams of the apparition. The words of his prayer were causing the being to cry out as if in pain. Just as it reached the table it disappeared with its cries echoing throughout the cottage.

"Look!" Tyler's eyes were fixed on the upper part of the wall. There, a red liquid oozed from where the wall and the ceiling met. It flowed down the wall, staining the collage of pictures red, then puddled on the floor.

Peter felt his head being pulled backward, his chin pointed to the ceiling. His eyes closed, yet as before, he could still see what was going on around him. He spoke, but not with his own voice. From the look on Tyler's face, she knew it was Gregory who was speaking through him.

"YOU MUST STOP THEM."

"How?" the professor asked.

"FIND THE BOOK."

"What book?"

"PETER KNOWS."

Just as the words left his lips, Peter saw the candle being hurled across the room, and where it had been in the center of the table the surface began to pulsate and bulge. The protrusion grew and loomed over him, forming the figure of the Beast. The professor and Tyler were frozen in their seats, watching the form of the Beast as it danced ritually upon the table. Its clawed hand held a sickle. Peter sat as if paralyzed, with his head tipped back and throat exposed. The Beast lifted the sickle high in the air, preparing to behead Peter.

"God help us!" Tyler screamed.

A bright, white light appeared beside Peter in the form of an angel. It stretched forth a flaming hand between Peter and the Beast, and the Beast disappeared before their eyes, emitting an earsplitting shriek. Peter was released from his captor and he slumped over on the table. Tyler let go of the professor's hand as he rose to turn on the light. She leaned over Peter and began crying hysterically.

"Peter, are you okay? Answer me, please." She wept.

Peter opened his eyes and looked at her. "I'm sorry. We failed to find your brother."

"You're sorry? My God, I thought you were going to be killed!"

"And he might well have been had it not been for you crying out to God," the professor added.

Peter pushed himself up from the table and wrapped his arms around Tyler and gave her a warm hug. "Thank you for saving my life."

"It wasn't me. It was supreme intervention. I'll never doubt again."

Peter smiled. "Then it was all worth it."

Their songs of praise were interrupted by the sound of scratching at the door. They stood quietly, looking at one another, each making sure the sounds wasn't their own imagination. Finally, the scratching sound came again and they all turned and looked at the door. It was then that the professor walked to the door and opened it. "Well, it appears we have a visitor," he said cheerfully.

Peter and Tyler looked at one another curiously then went to the door to have a look. Tyler's face lit up. "It's Phoenix! Hi, boy," she said and threw open the door.

The dog looked weak and nearly starved to death, but he wagged his tail at the mention of his name. He sauntered in and laid down in front of the stove. His feet were bloodied and his nails were worn completely down.

"We'd better get him to the vet," the professor suggested.

"I'll help you," Peter said, bending down to pick up the dog, but his legs got shaky and he thought he was going down on the floor himself.

"Whoa there, cowboy," Tyler said as she grabbed his arm. "I think you'd better sit this one out."

"I think she's right, Peter," the professor seconded. "I can get the dog to the vet myself. It's late, but I know where the doc lives. I'll take good care of him."

Peter didn't have the strength to argue, he just nodded and sat down on the loveseat. Tyler helped the professor get the dog in his car, then she came back into the cottage and sat down beside Peter.

"Are you okay? You really had me worried," she said.

"I didn't know you cared," Peter told her. He was feeling stronger.

"Some psychic you are," she teased.

Peter got up from the loveseat. "Come on," he said, holding out his hand to help her up. "I'll help you clean up this mess." He looked down at the puddles of red at the base of the walls. It was a testament. Proof of what had happened there that night.

It was nearly one o'clock in the morning when they finished cleaning up the floor and Peter took the sponge from Tyler's hand and threw it down in the basin of water.

"I don't remember if I thanked you for saving my life tonight."

"Oh, you did."

"But did I do it properly?" He closed the gap between them. So close it was hard for him to tell if it was his heart he could hear pounding, or hers. His lips pressed softly against hers and he was truly lost in the moment. She melted against him and it was at that moment that he believed he had always loved her. Her lips parted, welcoming him, but he pulled himself away. He could see the confusion in her eyes.

"Is something wrong?" she asked.

"No. It's just late, and we're both tired," he said as he turned away. He could feel her still staring at him as he turned off the light and sat down on one end of the loveseat. She finally crossed the room and laid down on the opposite end. They both closed their eyes, but sleep was a long time coming.

CHAPTER 8–EVE OF DESTRUCTION

Peter woke before dawn and made coffee. He poured himself a cup, and as he sat sipping it he thought about the dream he'd had after his swim the day before.

He somehow felt connected to the church in his dream and now he felt compelled to find it. Perhaps the professor would be able to help him.

He left Tyler a note. He didn't want her to wake and find him gone with no explanation. She'd think he was still running from her as he had the night before. It was crazy for him to pull away from her as he did. He knew it, even as he did it, but couldn't help himself. Hopefully the note would put her mind at ease. He propped the note up on the table, then went out the door and straight to the professor's house.

He knocked on the door for a good five minutes before the old man woke up and let him in. He directed Peter to a church on Pleasant Street in Brunswick. It was the only one around that he knew of with red doors. He said it was a Pentecostal church, founded around the year 1950 by a farm girl by the name of Madeline Heath. Her brothers had even helped build the church. Peter smiled as he went on and on about it. Jim always was a history buff.

Peter asked him to tell Tyler where he'd gone and that he'd be back by the end of the day if God be willing. The professor assured him he'd give her the message and if he didn't return by dusk he would suggest to Tyler that she spend the night at his place. Peter breathed a silent relief that Tyler wouldn't be alone at night in that cottage and thanked him for his generosity. Peter could see in the old man's eyes a curious stare, and knew he was almost tempted to ask why he needed to find this church with the red doors, but the old man just patted him on the shoulder and announced he was going back to bed. Peter watched him turn and walk to his bedroom. He stood there, alone in the kitchen, and wondered himself why he must find this particular church. Then he turned off the kitchen light, shut the door carefully behind him, and headed for Brunswick.

He found the place easily with the directions the professor had given him. He parallel parked right in front of the place and got out of the car. He stood in front of the church half expecting the door to swing open by itself and a voice invite him in as had happened in his dream. When that didn't happen, he smiled at himself, shook his head, then walked up the steps and went inside.

The church looked even smaller on the inside. It had maybe ten rows of long wooden pews with an aisle on each side and one down the center that led straight to the altar. There was an old upright piano down front on the right side and on the left a shiny black organ with duel keyboards. On the platform behind the pulpit were three crushed red velvet chairs. The one in the center had a higher back than the other two, and Peter surmised it was the one the minister sat in before his sermon. In front of the altar was a pair of well worn, wooden crutches and a leg brace attached to a scuffed up, brown shoe. Peter walked down the aisle toward the altar. There wasn't a soul to be seen, and every step he took echoed in the empty building. It was so quiet there that he could hear the rustling of his clothing with his slightest movement, and occasionally, a tractor trailer truck as it passed on Pleasant Street. Then he heard the tapping.

He turned and saw the silhouette of a figure standing in the rays of the sunlight that filled the door's archway. The person seemed to stand there, staring at him, for an eternity, then the tapping began again and the figure stepped out of the light and into his sight. It was an old woman, and she was blind. She had a light blue kerchief wrapped around her head and she wore a plain gray dress trimmed in old white lace that hung down to the tops of her high, laced up brown shoes. She walked a bit bent over with her cane darting back and forth in front of her, touching the end of every pew she passed as she made her way down the center aisle to Peter. She stopped just inches in front of him.

"I've been expecting you," she said.

The words hit Peter like a bolt of lightning. Her voice was the same as the person's voice in his dream. It filled him with peace and made him feel safe.

"Let us pray, Peter." She used her cane to help her kneel at the altar and motioned for him to join her.

Slowly he bent down beside her, not once taking his eyes off of her. He listened as she began to pray. The words seemed to flow from her lips. Never had he heard a prayer come so directly from the heart. There was something about the way she prayed that stirred him. Something that told him that God was hearing every word she said. Then suddenly, he realized she was no longer speaking English. She was speaking in a heavenly tongue that came from the very center of her soul and rolled effortlessly off her tongue, spreading a tone of worship throughout the small church. Though Peter didn't know what she was saying, he knew it was of God, for his spirit was witnessing with hers.

The old woman rose to her feet and stretched forth a hand and touched Peter's forehead. An enormous energy came through her hand and into him, giving him a jolt of power from on high. It knocked him backwards and he laid sprawled across the thin red carpeting in front of the altar. The blind woman continued to pray. She walked around him and stopped near his shoulder. She bent down beside him, and reached out a sure hand and picked up a small bottle of oil and coated the tip of her index finger. She reached out and, without site or fumbling, made the sign of the cross on Peter's forehead with the anointing oil. Peter closed his eyes and accepted his blessing, unable–and un-wanting–to stop the tears that rolled down his face. Hours went by, and the praying and the praising of God never ceased. Then at last, the old woman brought forth a message in tongues. The words were not understandable for Peter, any more than when she was praying in tongues, though he could tell a difference in the way the words were spoken. This was–

without a doubt–a message from God. She became silent after the message was brought forth and waited, praying that the interpretation wouldn't be quenched.

When the translation came it didn't come from the blind woman. It came to him. It flooded his heart and mind like a rushing tide and it stirred a mighty wind that came at him from all sides at once, engulfing him completely with the presence of the Holy Ghost. The voice told him of the battle to come. It would be the fight of his life, with the fate of souls, including his own, depending on the outcome. Peter then opened his eyes as he felt someone help him to his feet. It was the old woman.

"Peter, hold out your hand," she said.

He did as she asked, and she placed in his hand two small fonts. They were two glass vials, not more than two inches long. They contained a liquid.

"This vessel contains holy water," she said, tapping the container with her index finger, "and this one, contains Chrism, a concentrated oil used in baptisms."

"How shall I use them?" Peter asked.

"The answers are within you, Peter. This even I can see." She turned away from him and the tapping began as she made her way back down the aisle and out the door of the church.

Peter went straight out behind her, but she was gone. He looked left and right, but there wasn't a sign of her anywhere. Her exit was as mysterious as her entrance. He didn't feel it was his right to question. He was, however, sure of two things. God had sent her to him and it was He that had called her away.

He looked at his watch. If he left right now he could be back at the cottage by three in the afternoon. That would give him time. Time to find Gregory.

He drove a little over the speed limit, but he thought God would forgive him, considering what he was about to do. There was no turning back now. He had picked up the sword. He was going to confront evil, head on. When he arrived at the cottage he found Tyler and the professor sitting on the loveseat. He thought he saw a look of relief in Tyler's eyes as he walked through the door.

"I told her you'd be back," the professor said.

"And you were right." She smiled, then got up and walked over to the stove. The shiny aluminum coffee pot sat on the back burner with a blast of perked coffee splashing in its bubble. "Want a cup?" she asked Peter as she lifted the pot off the stove.

"Sure. A cup of coffee sounds good about now," he replied.

"Jim, could I warm your cup for you?" she asked.

"No thank you, dear. I've had my quota for today," he said. "I'll be shaking like a leaf as it is. I don't want to alarm my clients." He looked at his watch. "Speaking of which, I have an appointment in about fifteen minutes. Sorry kids," he said as he rose from the loveseat, "but this old buzzard has work to do."

"Be nice, Mr. Fortune Teller, and only tell the customer what they want to hear," Peter teased.

"Whatever pays the rent, my boy." He laughed and left the cottage.

Tyler poured herself another cup of coffee and sat

down again. He could tell she was dying to ask him questions about where he had been, why he had gone, and why he had left her, yet she was avoiding making eye contact. He loved teasing her like this. Making her wait was good for her.

"Any word about the dog?" he asked.

"Oh, yes. That's one of the things that Jim came to tell me. The vet wants to keep him for a few days. He's got a nasty infection, but he thinks Phoenix has a good chance of beating it. He's quite optimistic that he'll recover."

"Oh," Peter said with a smirk on his face, "so that's what you two were talking about when I came in."

"You're a curious one, aren't you?" she said and then sipped her coffee in an attempt to hide her own smirk.

"I'm not alone, am I?" he teased. "Why don't you just ask me, Tyler?"

"Ask you what?"

"About where I've been. You know it's killing you to find out."

"I don't want to pressure you." Now she sounded more serious.

"Let me guess, 'Peter will talk when he's ready.' Is that what Jim told you?"

"Something like that. He's extremely loyal to you. I was always pretty good at interviews. I've been told I have a knack for pulling information out of a person without them even realizing they're spilling their guts to me. Not so with your devoted friend. I know now as much as I did before. Not nearly enough, Mr. Amado." She leaned a little closer to him and whispered, "Not nearly enough."

"I'm what you see, Tyler. Nothing more. I am just a man."

"No, Peter. You're not just a man. I think I knew that the first moment I saw you. And after last night, well," she let out a faint laugh and shook her head, "Be honest, we both know 'just any man' would have taken advantage of me–given the fact that I wanted him to. Yet, you pulled away. Why?"

"There's a time and place for everything, Tyler."

"Is that anything like, 'All good things come to those who wait'?"

Peter smiled. "Perhaps."

She looked harder at him. "There's definitely something different about you, Peter. I noticed it when you came in just now," she said as she pulled her head to the side and lifted her chin, making motion toward the door as she glanced at it then back at him.

"You're very perceptive," he said smiling.

"What happened to you today?" She turned on the loveseat and looked at him square in the eyes. "What happened at that church?"

"So he did tell you," Peter was a bit surprised.

"Not everything. Only that you were asking about a church with red doors. Quite puzzling, actually. I can only assume you found it. Or did it find you?"

Peter only smiled.

"Well, are you going to tell me about it?"

"I was–reborn," he answered. He could feel the joy well up within him. "That's the only way I can describe it. I feel new. More alive than I have ever been."

"It shows. I can see it in your eyes."

"I learned a lot today, and you know, even though I know this is going to be the fight of my life, I feel I'm ready. Ready to do battle."

"With who?"

"With *them.*" The words came out of him before he could stop them. He saw Tyler's mouth drop open, and she shivered.

"You're talking about the two remaining coven members, aren't you?" She didn't wait for a response. Her face told him she knew the answer. "You don't seriously believe it's possible for someone to live over three hundred years." Her voice got shrilly. "Peter? Do you?"

"Satan has great power, though God has the greater. They battle for souls to fill their kingdoms. Nothing is impossible."

"Oh. Come on. Now be serious, Peter"

"Look, all I know is, without realizing it, your brother unleashed something so evil and demonic that it's going to take all of our faith combined to send it back to hell." Peter's face was stern.

"You *do* believe they live," she said solemnly. Peter could hear the disappointment in her voice to learn that he could believe something so outrageous.

"I believe that he that is within them, lives."

"Who?"

"Satan."

"My God, Peter, can you hear yourself? You're talking about doing battle with the devil. This is all so preposterous!" She shook her head, then rubbed her temples. "Even if you are right…"

"Surely you can't doubt that good and evil exists. Not after last night, you can't."

"Okay, okay, I believe," she admitted, "but you're talking about doing battle with Satan, for crying out loud! How do you expect any of us to come out of this unscathed?"

"The answer is in the book. When I find the book, I'll know how to fight him."

"Yeah, right. Lest we forget. The book in your dream. A *dream*, Peter."

"Oh, the book is real alright. It's what Greg was looking for the day he and Phoenix hiked along the shoreline. He found it, Tyler, and he paid for it with his life."

Her eyes welled up with tears and her voice got shaky. "And just what do you think will happen to you when you find it? I'll tell you. You're going to end up dead, just like my brother!"

Peter scooted closer to her on the loveseat and put his arm around her. "That won't happen."

"Promise?"

"Sh … I promise."

She pulled away from him and took a deep breath. "Then I'm going with you," she said matter-of-fact.

It caught Peter by surprise. "You're going to do

what?"

"I'm going with you to help find the book."

"I don't think that's such a good idea, Tyler. I mean, the book isn't all we're likely to find."

"You're talking about my brother now, aren't you?"

"Yes. Maybe you shouldn't be there."

"I have to go," she said firmly.

For a moment her eyes looked desperate. Like Maria Rosario's, and like the woman's in that apartment outside of Buffalo. Peter closed his eyes briefly and turned his head, trying to shake the thoughts from his mind. Then he stood.

"Let's go then." He outstretched his hand to her. She took it and he pulled her up off the loveseat, and they went out the door.

They hiked north, along the shoreline. The tide was high, and at times they had to move further inland to avoid getting wet. They passed four cottages along the way, none of which appeared to be occupied. So even if Gregory had screamed during his murder, there would have been no one to hear him. The rocky shore widened and they were able to step out of the bushes. Tyler was in front of Peter, and she stopped dead in her tracks. He nearly walked right into her.

"What's the matter, Tyler?" She stood unmoving. He came out of the bushes and walked around her to face her. "Tyler?" She was looking down at her feet. Peter dropped his eyes and saw her dismay. There was a bloody paw print on the ledge.

"Do you think it is Phoenix's print?" she asked.

"I have no reason to think otherwise." He lifted his eyes and looked around them. There was something familiar about the place. "Come on," he said as he took Tyler's hand and pulled her away. "Let's go on a bit further. We're close. I can feel it."

"And that's supposed to make me feel better?" She gripped his hand tighter.

They walked for about five more minutes. The shoreline had curved, blocking their view of the last cottage they had passed. Peter stopped suddenly and Tyler gasped.

"This is it." He felt Tyler go rigid. "Look," he said, pointing down to the ground at the edge of the trees. Several bloody paw prints could be seen on the rocks and on the grass at the base of the trees.

"It looks as though he pranced around," Tyler observed.

"Probably undecided."

"Undecided about what?"

"Whether to get help or to stay with his master."

She sucked in a gulp of air. "I feel dizzy."

"Here," Peter said, easing her down, "sit here for a while. I knew it was a bad idea for you to come."

She took several deep breaths. "No. I'll be alright." She got to her feet. "Let's go on."

Peter looked at her for a long time, like a coach trying to make sure his player was ready to get back into the game. He had seen the murder. He knew it was gruesome. He sure hoped she was ready for what they might find. He had to face it. The lady had a mind of her own. She was going to take every step that he did. He could see that.

"Alright, but let me go ahead. Okay?"

She nodded in agreement.

They entered the woods where the paw prints had ended, finding only a few smudges here and there to guide them on their way. It was terribly overgrown, but they made their way through the thicket, until they came out into a clearing in front of a stone shelter. Cautiously, they approached the door.

"Look!" Tyler covered her mouth with her hand and pointed at the bottom half of the door. There were long, deep scratches in the wood, stained a rusty red.

"I guess we have our answer of how Phoenix ended up with bloody paws," Peter concluded.

"He must have spent hours digging at that door. But why? You saw him. He was nearly starved to death. I could understand if the marks were on the inside of the door and he was trying to get out, but why was he trying to get in?"

"He was trying to be with the only person he knew that could take care of him."

"Oh, God. Greg," she cried and backed away from the door.

"Phoenix must have scoured the village trash cans for what little food he could find to keep him alive." Peter thought aloud.

"And always returning here, trying to get to Greg," she added.

"Let me go in first," Peter said. "You'll be okay here by yourself?"

She nodded, trying to fight back the tears, and motioned for him to go in.

Slowly he went back to the door and turned the knob. When the door opened and he stepped inside, he was amazed at how the house, despite the summer heat, had kept its chill. The small shelter had only one room, and there were years of accumulated dirt and dried leaves scattered around on the floor. Except for one area of the floor where the dirt and leaves had been brushed away. Peter got down on his hands and knees for a closer look and discovered a trap door. He worked the tips of his fingers into the cracks and managed to lift the wooden section and slid it off to one side. A putrid odor radiated up and out of the hole and disseminated throughout the room. Peter's heart throbbed in his chest as he looked down into the darkness. He didn't know what he had expected, perhaps something to jump up at him and pull him down. But nothing happened. He couldn't see anything except a dirt floor.

Tyler was calling to him from the outside. He could tell from her voice that she was getting more nervous by the second. He had to go back out and console her, if for nothing else but to keep her from coming in and discovering what he surmised was in the pit. He slid the trap door back over the hole, then went outside.

When he came out of the shelter and made eye contact with Tyler, it was as if her legs went to jelly and she sat straight down on the ground at the edge of the clearing. She removed her hands from her mouth and held them tightly together as she bent forward and placed them between her knees. It was as though the act was keeping them from flailing and her legs from carrying her away from the dreadful scene. He could tell the words came hard, but she asked them.

"Did you find anything?"

"Not yet," he told her, shaking his head. "There's a dugout beneath the place, but not enough light to see. I'll have to go down. Maybe once my eyes adjust to the darkness I'll be able to see if we're on the right track."

"I'll go with you," she said. Her voice caught in her throat and the last of her sentence came out as a whisper.

"No!" He blocked her path as she tried to walk around him and held her by her shoulders.

Her eyes found his. "What's with you, Peter? I just want to have a look. I have excellent night vision. Maybe I can help so we can get the heck out of here."

"No, Tyler," he shook his head, "don't go in."

"Why not?" Her eyes watered. "Is he in there?" She bit her lower lip, then pulled away from him and darted into the building.

"Tyler, no!" He followed her inside. She stood in the center of the room with her hands covering her nose and mouth. She looked as if she was going to be sick. Peter again took her by the shoulders, only this time he forced her from the building and sat her down next to a tree and held her tightly.

"Listen to me, Tyler, we don't know for sure that it's Greg down there. It could be anything. A sick animal could have crawled down there to die, or a hunter could have gutted a deer down there and left its remains to rot. You know how closed up spaces can harbor odors from years ago," he rambled on.

"Or it could be the body of my brother down there. Couldn't it?"

His eyes locked with hers. "Yes. It could be Greg."

He could see the pain in her eyes. He knew what she was going through. He had lost his brother, too. Daniel was only nine years old when he fell into the pit they had dug that summer so long ago. He remembered finding him, lying in the dirt at the bottom of the hole. He had broken his neck. The guilt of that fateful day and his inability to protect him from the fall came flooding into his mind. They had been racing that day and Peter ran in the direction of the hole. The grass in the field had grown up around the edges of the empty pool, and Peter never thought that Daniel would forget it was there. But he did. He was a blur as he passed Peter with a broad smile on his face and plunged head first into the pit. Peter had never forgiven himself for running in that direction, and he didn't believe he ever could. He was older than Daniel by three years. He was supposed to be his brother's keeper, and he failed. Just as he had failed with that little boy outside of Buffalo.

"Peter?" Tyler called him back to the present. "Are you alright?"

He shook his head of the memories. "Yeah. I'm fine." The words stuck in his throat. He knew that wasn't entirely true. "I'm going back in. Wait here."

He reentered the stone shelter and slid the trap door off of the opening. He reeled from the smell that emanated from the pit. It was the smell of rotting flesh and something else—a musty, earthy odor, just as he had smelled in his dream. It was the same smell that was in his clothing after his vision at the house on Flintridge Drive, and on that horrible day when he pulled his brother's limp body out of the pit they had dug in the field behind their house. He tried to put the past behind him as he leaned over the hole in the floor. He shielded his eyes from the light rays that shined into the room and tried to get a better look below. As his eyes adjusted to the darkness, he could see a crude ladder made of tree limbs with most of the bark still intact. Carefully, he swung his legs over the hole in the floor, braced a hand on each side of the opening, and lowered his feet down to the first rung of the ladder. Slowly he eased his full weight on the rung and began his decent into the darkness.

Once he was standing on the dirt floor, he turned slowly around, and strained to see as much of the dugout as possible. He could hear the beating of his heart in his ears as he realized there was movement just ahead of him. He stepped to the side, out of the ray of light that streamed down through the opening above him. Then he saw them. Two black robed figures walking back and forth, seemingly unaware of his presence. He thought this must be a vision, yet he hadn't felt the tug. He stood still, vaguely aware of Tyler calling down to him. The forms paced back and forth in front of a makeshift altar and performed some sort of ritualistic dance. Peter stayed completely silent, observing the black robed figures. He hadn't noticed that Tyler had come down the ladder and was standing on the last rung.

"Can they see us?" she whispered.

Peter jumped half out of his skin. His reaction startled her, too, and she gasped and gripped the ladder even tighter causing her knuckles to go white.

"You can see them, too?"

Tyler could only nod her head as a reply. Her eyes were transfixed on the two black robed figures, who now stopped their dancing and stood with their backs turned to Peter and Tyler. They began to chant in a strange tongue that sent shivers down Peter's back. Their torsos nodded in rhythm like a praying rabbi, then they moved in unison to a corner in the dark room. There, they anointed a candle with oil and it flamed, casting their shadows up on the wall.

The candle light illuminated the altar, and Peter could see the book. It was as if it was calling to him, telling him to come and pick it up. It seemed he had no control of his legs as he moved toward the altar. He could hear Tyler saying no, don't go, but he couldn't help himself. He had to have the book. He reached the altar and picked it up, clutching it to his chest.

The two black forms continued to chant. Their voices rose in pitch and got louder and louder, until the words were indistinguishable and the volume so intense Peter thought he and Tyler would lose their hearing. Then suddenly they stopped and the absence of sound was also deafening. Peter tried to walk toward Tyler with the book, but he couldn't move his legs. He was being held by an invisible force. He yelled to Tyler to get out, but she was frozen as well. Her eyes were glued to an area of the dugout from where there came a faint sound. It was a scuffing sound, coming from the darkest corner of the room. Someone or *something* was moving toward her. She stared, intently, into the darkness as a bloody form emerged. She hooked her right arm through the rung of the ladder and covered her mouth with her left hand to stifle a scream as the figure stepped out into the light. It was Gregory.

He had a grotesque wound on the right side of his

neck, and his throat looked as if it had been chewed away. His tongue protruded from a slit, giving the appearance of a mini necktie. His mouth worked to form words as he limped toward her, dragging the lower part of his nearly severed left leg. The foot was turned backwards and it was laying on its side as he dragged it across the dirt floor. "Please, don't let him take the book," he pleaded with her. "It is mine. My life for the book. Don't let him take it from me, Ty."

Peter tried to go to her, but he was still unable to move. He yelled, "Don't listen to it, Tyler! It's not your brother. Greg is dead."

Tyler cried hysterically, torn between the horror that surrounded her and the love she had for her brother. She stepped down the ladder and stood flatfooted on the dirt floor, facing him. Tears streamed down her cheeks as she wrapped her arms around herself.

"Don't listen to it. It's a demon using him. Can't you see that?" Peter shouted at her. "Think, Tyler! Use your head. He can't speak to you. He has no throat, for God's sake! Don't listen. It's them! They're using him."

The demon within the corpse became angry and its pace increased toward Tyler. Peter desperately cried out for God to help him, and the unseen chains that held him were broken from him and he was free. He dashed toward Tyler, placing his body between her and her brother's corpse. He pleaded for the blood of the precious Lamb of God to cover them and protect them from all evil, and the body of Gregory Moore lost its mobility and it dropped to the dirt floor with a thud.

Peter turned Tyler around and shoved her up the ladder and didn't stop until they were both outside the stone shelter. Peter pulled her close to him with the book wedged tightly between them.

"Let's get out of here," Peter told her. He half expected the two robed figures to burst from the building at any moment and tear them limb from limb. But that didn't happen, and every step they took that led them away from that place was a victory. Peter praised God all the way back to the cottage, with one arm holding the book and the other wrapped tightly around Tyler, who was clearly in shock.

Once inside the cottage, Peter helped Tyler over to the loveseat and she sat down in a daze. He wrapped the lap blanket around her and got her a glass of water. He held it to her lips and she took a couple of sips. It seemed to snap her out of it a little bit as she closed her eyes and laid against the arm of the loveseat. He sat down beside her and finally let out his breath. He was just winding down when a knock came at the door. He nearly jumped out of his skin, thinking the demons had come for him. They hadn't. It was the professor.

"Sh," Peter hushed him as he let him in. Tyler seemed to be resting comfortably.

"What in God's name happened?" he whispered to Peter. "I saw you two pass my place. Is she alright?"

"I don't know, Jim. We found her brother. It wasn't pretty."

"My God! The poor thing," he said, looking down at her. "What a terrible thing to go through."

"You don't know the half of it, my friend." Peter took a swig of Tyler's water, then made a motion for the professor to step out of earshot of Tyler. He took the book from under his shirt.

"You found it!"

"And that's not all. The two remaining coven members were there, too."

"What! Where?"

"There's a stone shelter up the shore. There's a dugout beneath it. That's where we found her brother and the book. And them."

"Impossible!"

"Not unless we were both having the same nightmare," Peter said. He passed the book to the professor. "Perhaps we're hallucinating right now, huh, Jim? I don't know. Feels real. You tell me." He looked at the professor with wide, unblinking eyes.

The professor swallowed hard, then opened the book. "My, my, my," he said over and over.

"Can you translate it?"

"I don't know. It will take some time."

"Well, we don't have much time, my friend. They know we have it. No one is safe." He looked at Tyler, asleep on the loveseat. "I don't want to put her through any more trauma. I don't know how much more she can take."

"I understand, Peter," he replied, gesturing with the book, "I'll get right on it." He turned to leave, but before doing so he turned to Peter again and said, "I don't understand how the two of you got out of there alive with the book."

"Neither do I," Tyler spoke up, yet her voice sounded weak. It was evident, she was in shock.

"Ah, little missy, you're awake," the professor said with a smile.

"How *did* we get out of there, Peter?"

The professor butted in. "I think your brother's spirit was looking out for you."

"But what about Peter?"

"Oh, that's easy…" the professor began to say, but Peter cut him off.

"Professional trickery," Peter teased her. "I've learned to go unseen."

"Ha. Ha." She wasn't buying it. "So, what's the real scoop, Professor?"

He opened his mouth to answer her, but Peter placed an arm around his shoulders and rushed him to the door. He pressed the book to his chest. "I think you've got a lot of work to do. Isn't that right, Professor?" Peter kept his back to Tyler and kept nodding his head until the professor gave in and nodded his head with him. Some things he still didn't want Tyler to know. Not yet. He hurried the old man out the door and bid him a goodnight as he went down the path.

"What was that all about?" she questioned him, clearly confused.

Peter went to her and placed the tip of his index finger on the wrinkle between her brows. "Surely you know scowling can bring on wrinkles."

She smiled and punched him in the gut with the back of her hand. "Oh, stop it. You're as bad as–Gregory." Her smile faded.

"I'm sorry. The last thing I wanted was to remind

you of him."

"You didn't. Fact is, I'll never forget." She shuddered. "What happened this afternoon, Peter? You, know I have a fear of small enclosures. I don't know what compelled me to go down into that hole, but it was so strong. Before I even knew what was happening I was halfway down the ladder. It was as if I couldn't stop. Tell me it was all a bad dream. That it couldn't have happened the way I remember it."

Peter wished he could, but he couldn't. Instead, he held her close until she went to sleep.

Two hours passed. It was nearly seven-thirty. Peter heard the professor coming up the steps, and eased his arm out from under Tyler and laid her head down gently on the back of the loveseat. Quickly he went to the door before the professor could knock. He stepped outside, leaving the door ajar, not wanting the squeaking hinges to wake her. The old man looked as if he had just heard of the death of a loved one.

"What is it, Jim?"

"It's worse than we ever imagined." His voice was hoarse and shaky.

"What do you mean?"

"I've translated the book." He swallowed hard and wiped his mouth with the side of his hand, leaving his bushy mustache disheveled.

"And?" Peter could feel a tightening in his chest.

"It's written in a language once spoken by a Mexican Indian tribe thought to be merely a myth. Legend has it, those who spoke the strange tongue–a language made up of several tongues actually–were considered to be 'the evil ones.' A people that would lay down their lives for Satan."

"So you think we're dealing with some sort of medicine man? Is that it?"

"No. But I do think we're dealing with someone or something that was powerful enough to make that tribe only a story in history."

"What *does* it say, Jim?"

"The book tells of a coven that occupied Salem over three hundred years ago. The High Priestess, a wicked woman named Mary Deven, was impregnated by Satan himself. She begat him a daughter. Satan named her Sarah. The name is Hebrew, Peter. It means Princess. Mary was given enormous power to watch over Satan's offspring. They were sealed up in a pit to wait until the appointed time. Only Gregory Moore unleashed them when he opened their hideaway."

"They are the forms we saw in the dugout."

"Yes. And there's more. Much more."

Peter felt a shiver run through him at the prospect of what the old man was going to say next. He couldn't even ask him to continue. He only stared at him, waiting for him to reveal what he had learned. What had caused his skin to become as gray as his bushy mustache?

"Peter, Sarah is to give birth to the antichrist. She was born with Lucifer's seed."

Peter was stunned at what he was hearing, though deep in his gut he knew, yes he knew, it was true. Satan loved to mock God. It was his greatest joy. He would soon unleash his demon son on the world, a Christ of sorts, a descendant of Mary.

"How can we fight this, Jim? It is written."

"I know you don't want to hear this, but I think we should fight fire with fire."

"I'm listening."

"Sarah hasn't come to full power. If we were to perform an exorcism on her ..."

"No! I don't want to go through that hell again." Peter raised his voice, then remembering Tyler, tried to control himself.

The professor grabbed Peter by the front of his shirt, forcing him to listen. "It may be our only chance. Perhaps by doing so, we can evoke Satan's wrath on Mary and send them both back to hell."

Peter was feeling sick.

"I'm as sorry about that little boy as you are, Peter. It was an awful experience. We'll never be able to change that."

"It was 'an awful experience'?" He mocked with a forced smile. "It was tragic!" he now shouted, then stifled himself to a hoarse, strained whisper. "That little boy was smeared all over that ceiling, Jim. It took days to scrape him off of it."

"Before the force killed him, he turned back from that horrible demon, and became a little boy again, looking into his mother's eyes, and asking forgiveness. Remember *that,* Peter. At least we have *that.*"

"But that mother has no son. We failed."

"No, Peter. If you truly believe in God, you can't believe that. Michael was saved in the only way that truly matters."

"I don't know if I can do that again," Peter said.

"I can't do it alone. I need you. We need each other."

Peter could see there would be no swaying the old man this time, and he was sure his sigh told the old man he'd won.

"Come now, let's go inside and tell Tyler what we're going to do," the professor said.

Peter caught him by the arm as he tried to pass him to enter the cottage. "Michael isn't the only little boy I've been thinking a lot about lately."

The professor nodded and patted the back of Peter's hand. He knew him like a son and could feel his heart being torn from him. If only there were words to ease the pain, but there were none. "Daniel?"

Peter turned his back to him and sighed. "That dugout beneath the stone shelter, the smell of dirt ..." His voice cracked and he clinched his teeth and looked at the ocean.

The professor got behind him and placed an arthritic hand on his shoulder. He leaned into him and spoke with a low, whispering voice. "Satan knows your weaknesses, Peter, and he'll use them against you if you let him. Don't let him. Daniel is at rest. You be strong. You hear me, boy?" He patted Peter's shoulder twice.

Peter took a deep breath and nodded. He knew his old friend was right. Why couldn't he shake this feeling of guilt for his brother's death? He straightened and turned to face his old friend. He smiled at him, but was sure the professor could see through the tears in his eyes as he quickly turned and led them into the cottage.

Tyler woke up and sat up on the loveseat as soon as they walked in, giving the professor room to sit down. Peter went to the stove to make coffee. Tyler sat without saying a word, apparently listening to Peter and the professor make small talk. Then she interrupted them.

"How is it that place has stayed secret for so long? Why is it that no one has found them before this?"

"This village has always been highly superstitious for as far back as the history books can take you," the professor explained. "Quite frankly, it's why I settled here. Business has really been great for me." That got a chuckle out of Tyler and Peter, and the professor smiled. Then his face turned serious again. "Legends around here has it that the stone shelter belonged to a hunter who came up missing some centuries ago. There have been those that say they have seen his ghost and that he still haunts the woods around the stone house. Makes sense to me–knowing the villagers as I do–that no one around here has poked around the place. Then there was that family--their names escape me at the moment—but I remember it being a time that caused a great many to fear being out alone in those woods."

"What happened to the family?" Tyler asked.

"They were all brutally murdered. As I remember the story, the oldest daughter had been spending time with her grandmother and had returned home only to find them all dead. It was rumored that it was a wild animal that had attacked them. Many claimed to have seen their ghosts in those woods, and avoided the area as best they could."

"Can't say that I blame them. I, for one, will take ghost stories a little more seriously from now on," Tyler remarked.

"Well, we hope to put this ghost story to rest very soon," Peter added as he passed them each a cup of coffee.

"I'm afraid to ask," Tyler said under her breath, then sipped from her cup.

"We're going to perform an exorcism tonight," the professor told her.

She nearly choked on her coffee and began to cough to clear her throat. She tried to speak and her voice was raspy. "An exorcism?" She managed to get out the words. "You mean like in the movie, 'The Exorcist'? That kind of exorcism?" Her eyes were wide, and she steadied her cup with both hands.

"Well, no pea soup or spinning heads," the professor replied.

"At least we hope not," Peter said under his breath as he poured a little more coffee in his cup. The professor cleared his throat upon hearing that remark. "Look, Tyler, you don't have to go, you know. It would be better, actually, if you stayed here," Peter told her.

"No way!" She got up and walked to the side board and sat her cup down, then folded her arms across herself. "I'm not staying here alone. I may never stay anywhere alone ever again!" She shivered.

"You could stay at Jim's. Couldn't she?" Peter looked at the professor for support.

"No," she said firmly. "I'm going with you."

"She might be right, Peter. She may be too vulnerable here. At least if she's with us we'll have a chance to protect her."

"That's right." She nodded and went back to the loveseat to sit again beside the professor, placing an arm around his shoulders. Then she scowled at him. "Protect me from who?"

"The Beast," the professor said as a matter of fact.

"What...beast?" she asked. The color drained from her face.

"Satan." The answer came out of Peter so fast he couldn't stop himself. Once it was spoken aloud it sounded so absurd that a chuckle spilled out of him and he quickly stifled it, covering his mouth with the forefinger of his left hand.

"Wait just a minute," Tyler said, "we're going to perform an exorcism on Satan?"

"Well, yeah, in a manner of speaking," the professor answered.

She looked from one to the other. "I don't think I'm going to like what comes out of him."

She sounded so serious, and even though they all knew the situation to be just that, it struck them all funny, and they all laughed together. It was something they all needed to release the tension, and it felt good. Peter knew she was right in a sense. They were going to be rebuking more than just a demon. They were going to be rebuking Satan himself. They were going to try to change what was written, and even he didn't know what would happen when they tried to do this. They were all going to require a strong spirit and a clear mind to bind the Beast and delay the antichrist's coming. They would take the next few hours to prepare themselves physically, emotionally, and spiritually, to confront Mary and Sarah Deven in the darkest hour–just before dawn.

And as it is appointed unto men once to die, but after this the judgment:

Hebrews 9:27

CHAPTER 9–THE APPOINTED LOT

The professor stood between Peter and Tyler and placed a hand on each of their shoulders. "Now listen, you two, enough of roughing it out here at the cottage. I insist you wait out the clock at my place." He looked at Tyler, "There's a nice warm bed with clean sheets just waiting for you. Now don't tell me that doesn't sound good to you."

Tyler looked at Peter. He could see the part about the sheets had won her over. "Looks like you've got company, old friend," he said.

"Then it's settled," the professor said with a smile, then he waved them out the cottage door.

Each had their shot at the shower, then Tyler busied herself with fixing them all something to eat. Peter and the professor went off to themselves and went over the rites they would be using to perform the exorcism. After dinner, Tyler retired to the long awaited sheets under the condition they would wake her when the time came to journey to the stone shelter. Only then did she agree to get some sleep.

Peter, on the other hand, elected not to rest. Instead, he found a room away from the others, and prayed. He knew the task ahead was going to require more than a rested body. He was going to need the strength that only God could give him. He knelt by his bedside and with his face pressed against the mattress he cried out for God to fill him. To enfold his soul with the holiest of light, that no darkness could enter in. His soul was hungry and he pleaded for God to fill it with the Holy Ghost and fire from on high so that he would be able to do battle with the forces of darkness. He had prayed for nearly an hour when his voice trailed off and he was close to sleep.

In that moment he felt a hand touch his shoulder. At first he thought it was Tyler, but then he heard a voice say, "Fear not, for I am with thee."

He jumped to his feet, turned and stumbled backward, sitting down with a plunk. His knee collided with his chin, but he didn't pay any attention to the pain. He stayed slumped with his back against the bed and his knees drawn up to his chest as he saw appear before him a bright, bluish white light. The second he looked into the light he was filled with peace and love and a joy he had never known before. He reached out with a shaky hand and touched the aura of the heavenly form, and was instantly compelled to fall on his face while in the presence of this divine being. He felt his soul being swept clean and an allover feeling of being reborn surged through his body. Then the spirit vanished as miraculously as it had appeared, but Peter wasn't troubled. He felt exhilarated from the top of his head to the soles of his feet. He knew that same light that had visited him this night now shined from within him, and that nothing could take that away. Not fear. Not sadness. Not even the darkness could touch him now. He was going into battle with evil, but he was not alone.

A knock came at the bedroom door, and he awakened.

"It's time to get started, Peter." It was the professor. His voice sounded muffled as he spoke through the door.

"Yes," Peter answered. "I'm ready."

He looked around the room, still dazed with sleep, his eyes lingering over the area where the Angel of Light had appeared to him. He heard the professor go back down the stairs, leaving him to wake Tyler. He wished he could just let her sleep until it was all over, but he had made a promise, so he got up and went to the room she was resting in. The door was left ajar and he gently knocked on the door casing. She stirred briefly, then snuggled down again. Peter went to the bed and sat himself down easily and watched her for a while. Her face looked so peaceful. No scowls, no pain, just full of the contentment she had found in her sleep. Reluctantly, he placed a hand on her shoulder and shook her gently as he called her name. She looked at him with eyes still full of sleep.

"Is it time already?" Her voice was a low raspy whisper.

Peter whispered back, "Yes. You can stay here, you know. I think you'd be safe here."

"No way!" She raised up on her elbows, fully awake now. "I'd go nuts worrying about you." Her eyes widened and she quickly added, "About both of you. I'd be worried about both of you."

He brushed the platinum blonde hair away from her face, then raised his left brow and tilted his head into a tantalizing pose before relaxing into a smile. "Okay. We'll be waiting downstairs." He pushed up off the bed and walked to the door.

"I'll only be a few moments," she said.

Peter raised a hand and formed an okay sign as he went out of the room and closed the door behind him. The professor was waiting for him at the foot of the stairs. He was pacing and wringing his hands. He looked up when he heard Peter descending the steps.

"Is she still coming with us?" he asked Peter. It was written all over his face. He wanted her to stay.

"You know it."

The professor shook his head. "That's one gutsy gal."

"Have you got everything ready that we'll need for the exorcism?" Peter asked.

The professor nodded and pointed to a duffle bag he had placed by the door. He was obviously unnerved by what they were about to do. His face looked drawn and there was a grayness about his complexion.

"Are you sure you're up for this, old man?"

"Don't worry about me. There's plenty of fight left in this old bird. It's you that I'm concerned about."

"Me? Why?"

"Satan knows your weaknesses, Peter, and he'll use them against you. You can take that to the bank."

"Not to worry, my friend, I've got help." Peter lifted a finger and pointed up.

"That's what I'm counting on." He motioned for Peter to follow him into the kitchen, out of earshot of Tyler. There he poured three cups of coffee and placed them on the table. The stairs creaked as Tyler came down them and the professor leaned in close to Peter. "I can't stress to you enough how important is it that you perform each rite exactly as the ages have dictated. It's not the time to ad-lib. Not with these two. And most of all, Peter, believe in your God, for it is He, and He alone, that will save us all from evil."

"Be of good cheer, Jim, for I abide with Him, and He with me." Peter could feel his own face aglow and could see in the old man's eyes that he was aware of it, too. It seemed to help the old man relax a bit and the color came back into his cheeks.

"You know, Peter," he said, not taking his eyes off of him, "for the first time, I think you might be right."

"First time? Come on, give me break, Professor." Peter winked. "Keep the faith."

Tyler walked into the kitchen and sat down in front of her cup of coffee. She looked more rested than either of them, but she hadn't witnessed an exorcism as they had. Peter even wondered if she remembered the horror they had witnessed upon seeing her brother beneath the stone shelter. She hadn't mentioned Greg. Only the stone shelter and the fact she didn't know how they made it out of there. He thought perhaps the shock of it had caused her to block it out. He wasn't going to press it. It was better if she didn't remember. When it was all over, Gregory would get a proper burial.

"Drink up, you two," the professor said as he raised his cup. "Dawn will be here before we know it."

They finished their coffee in silence, then Peter got up and walked around the table and stood behind Tyler. He reached into the front pocket of his jeans and pulled out a gold chain. Holding it by the clasp he reached around Tyler and let the emblem dangle in front of her face.

"Oh, what a beautiful cross!" she marveled.

"I'd like you to wear it," he said.

"Oh, no, I would be afraid of losing it. It looks so old. Is it a family heirloom?" She examined it more closely.

"Something like that. I would just feel better if you wore it." He could see she was hesitating. "At least until this whole ordeal is over. Please?"

She shrugged. "Okay. If it will make you feel better."

"It would," he said as he placed it around her neck and fastened the clasp.

"I really do wish you'd tell me where you got it, though. It's beautiful."

From the corner of his eye he saw the professor's lower lip drop away from his big, bushy mustache in order to answer Tyler's question. Peter cleared his throat to divert the professor's attention. He glanced up at Peter, and Peter shook his head. The professor promptly closed his mouth, and Tyler was none the wiser. Peter let out his breath. He couldn't help it. A part of him was reluctant to tell her where he had gotten the cross. He wasn't ready. Not yet.

"How about you, old man?" Peter held up another, yet smaller, cross.

"Ah, no cross for me, Peter," he said, waving it away. He reached into his shirt pocket and pulled out a scarab and held it up. "This stone beetle amulet has always brought me good luck and, since it is a symbol of destruction in Ancient Egypt, I feel quite safe with it in my possession."

"You know, Professor," Peter said, "sometimes I worry about you and your superstitions."

"Well, you have your faith and I have mine," he replied in a huff as he got up and put on his jacket. He grunted as he bent down to pick up the duffle bag, then he went out the door and the screen snapped shut behind him.

Peter and Tyler looked at one another with their mouths hanging open. "Well," Peter joked, "I guess that's our cue to go," Tyler let out a laugh so unrestrained it warmed him through and through. For a moment they both forgot about the evil that awaited them. Peter reached for her jacket and helped her put it on. His hands lingered on her shoulders and he had to fight the urge to pull her back toward him and hold her close. He had nearly lost the battle when she moved away from him and walked to the door. Just as she reached it he felt his arm extend, as if it had a will of its own, and grabbed her arm. She stopped, turned and leaned on the door casing. He stood opposite her in the archway still holding her around the arm.

"You don't have to go, you know," he said to her once more.

"And let you guys have all the fun? Not a chance,

Amado."

She started to push away from the door casing, but Peter took a step closer and closed the gap between them. "Look," Peter said. His voice became low, almost a whisper, and they were standing toe to toe, eye to eye, so close that he could feel the heat of her breath against his lips. "Things could get rough. I don't want to lose you." He could see in her eyes, she was as dizzy as he was, and the soft, tender gaze drew him closer still. His heart raced to keep up with his soul while their movements seemed to be in slow motion, until at last, he felt her lips on his, warm, wet, and much too inviting. It would have been easy for him to return her sweet kiss, but—

"Hey, you two," the professor yelled from halfway down to the shore, "hurry up before I lose my nerve." His voice echoed off other buildings in the stillness of the night.

They looked at the old man and laughed as they watched him turn and continue walking toward the ocean. Peter shook his head and smiled at himself, realizing how dear the old fellow had become to him. Then he looked back at Tyler and wanted so much to be lost in her gaze again. They both smiled at each other and placed their foreheads together, sharing one another's breath.

"Later?" she asked.

"Later." He saw her eyes sparkle and it made his knees weak. Then she pushed away from the door casing, rubbing up against him briefly before turning to go out the door. He watched her trot up behind the professor and give him a hug. He hoped he wasn't making a mistake by allowing her to come along. She was new to this diabolical game. The warmth he'd felt just seconds before was replaced by dread as he went out of the house and closed the door behind him. He reached into his pocket and made sure he still had the two fonts the blind woman had given him. He did. One containing oil, the other holy water. She had told him he would know when and how to use them, and he prayed she was right as he joined the professor and Tyler now standing by the sea.

The night was dead silent. As the villagers slept, the only sound that could be heard was the ocean waves lapping at the shore. Even that was muted by the bulbous seaweed that blanketed the rocks at the water's edge. The tide was out, enabling them to walk the entire distance without having to retreat to the woods, but it was a difficult walk. The professor slipped once on the moss covered rocks, but insisted he was alright and that they should go on without concern for him.

Peter stopped suddenly. "This is it. We're here."

Tyler looked at him in amazement. "Are you sure you weren't a Seeing Eye dog in some former life?"

"I don't need to see the place. I can feel it."

"If Peter says we're here, then we're here," the professor told her. "And might I add, thank the Lord in Heaven."

"I'll second that," Tyler agreed. "It takes some of the wonder out of why this place has remained hidden, doesn't it?"

"Sh," Peter placed a finger to his lips. He walked into the woods first, with Tyler holding tightly to the hem of his jacket. The professor followed behind her, cursing at the bushes that smacked him in the face as he wove through the overgrown brush. Soon they walked out into the clearing and stopped about twenty feet away from the stone shelter. There was an unnatural stillness in the air and an unearthly chill surrounded them.

"Peter," the professor whispered, "we must begin."

"Aren't we going in?" Tyler asked as she pulled the front of her jacket together and wrapped her arms around herself.

"There's no need. They know we are here," Peter told her. He saw the color drain from her face and tears fill her eyes.

The professor passed the duffle bag to Peter and for a moment they were caught in each other's stare, then Peter lowered his eyes and opened the bag. He removed a bell, a candle, and the Holy Bible. Tyler grabbed the side of the bag and peered inside. It was empty.

"Awe, you guys," she whined and pushed the bag away. "I'd thought you'd, at the very least, be carrying an Uzi in there! I really wish you'd get with the program!" She snapped. They didn't laugh and Peter knew she hadn't expected them to. He knew it was just her way of dealing with her fear of the unknown.

Peter made the sign of the cross and began to pray the Lord's Prayer. The professor and Tyler joined him and their voices grew in strength as they felt of one accord. Then from the bowels of the stone shelter came an agonizing scream that shattered the stillness of the night. They continued to pray, their voices rising in volume to be heard above the screams that came from the darkest depth of the stone shelter. As they concluded their prayer the door of the small building swung open ever so slowly. At first they saw no one, then in the next instant, Mary Deven was standing in the doorway.

She was horribly deformed. A growth protruded from the right side of her shoulder blade, giving her the appearance of one afflicted with a severe case of humpback. For the first time they could see her face. Her color was chalky, and her skin was scabrous and pitted with sores, some oozing a green-yellow puss. An odious stench emanated from her, making them all want to vomit from the putrid smell. The front of her skull had protruded, giving her an over-hanging brow that cast a black shadow beneath it. Her eyes had no pupils and were a milky white with blood-filled webs of bulging veins.

Peter held up the Holy Bible and she recoiled at the site of it. As she veered to the left, Peter saw movement behind her. It was Sarah, and her eyes glowed a bright green-yellow. Mary opened her mouth to speak and her voice filled the air around them.

"Give to us our Holy Book, then leave this place, and ye *may* live," Mary Deven growled at them.

The professor blew out a puff of air that lifted one side of his bushy mustache. He swore under his breath, scoffed at her threat, and held tightly to his amulet. Mary saw him clutching to his beliefs.

"Doth thou think I am afraid of a bug? Thou art a foolish man," she said angrily. She then lifted her arms and began to speak in an ungodly tongue, and Sarah chanted behind her.

A foul odor, worse than the first, filled the air, and caused Tyler to vomit. Peter wanted to help her, but feared diverting his attention was what Mary wanted more than anything else, so he fought his urges and opened the Holy Bible and began to read from its scriptures. A groan came from deep within Mary's throat as the book was opened and the words came forth, and her anger was manifested as the trees and the bushes were blown by a supernatural wind. Peter was not swayed by her diabolical display of power as he lit the candle. He glanced at the professor and Tyler, and could see they were both amazed that not only was he able to light the candle, but that it stayed lit. He was not. Bracing himself against the winds of hell, he read the ritual to exorcise Sarah of her witchcraft.

"We exclude him from the bosom of our Holy Mother the Church, and we judge him condemned to eternal fire with Satan and his angels and all the reprobate so long as he will not burst the fetters of the demon, do penance and satisfy the church." He closed the book, rang the bell–a symbolic toll for death–blew out the candle and threw it down on the ground, symbolizing the removal of the victim's soul from the sight of God.

Mary snarled, baring jagged, rotten teeth, and a froth flew from the corners of her mouth as Peter read the rite. Behind her they could see Sarah as her entire body began to convulse. A force not unlike that manifested by electricity, lifted her completely off the floor. Her bare feet patted against the floor of the stone shelter as her body shook violently. Her glowing, yellow eyes rolled up into her head, and a moan came from deep in her throat as her skin became as molten lava and maneuvered itself into the form of the Beast. Its eyes flashed open and it looked straight at Peter with such loathing and petulance that it made him cringe. Its horned head tilted back and it opened its mouth to roar, but all that came out was Sarah's shriek as she and he who dwelled within her were swallowed up by the darkness.

"NO!" Mary cried out. Her voice was so powerful it shook the ground they stood on.

"Yes!" the professor screamed back at her, clenching his teeth into a hiss.

Mary's voice then became a harsh whisper as she spewed her sentence. "So death shall reign."

She lifted her arms and it was as if all the air around them was sucked up in a vacuum and it roared overhead like the intake of a mighty jet engine. The sound was a barrier that pressed down upon them, restricting their movements and binding their spirit. It was much like the feeling Peter had experienced when he walked through the door of the house on Flintridge Drive, only more powerful. Like the extreme pressure of being submerged in deep water. He looked at Tyler and she stood with her mouth open and the palms of her hands pressed against the sides of her head.

The professor, still clutching to his amulet, was drawn by an unseen force toward Mary. The toes of his shoes dug into the ground as he tried desperately to stop his movement toward her. Peter heard Tyler scream, then realized he, too, was screaming for his release as he watched Mary deliver her vengeance. The professor coughed and a puff of smoke came out of his mouth. His skin began to smolder beneath his clothes and he screamed as he burst into flames. His cries of pain pierced Peter's heart and Peter yelled at the top of his lungs, trying to drown out the cries of agony coming from his dear old friend.

Only after Mary disappeared into the darkness of the stone shelter were Peter and Tyler released from her spell. Still in shock at what they had just witnessed, they ran to the professor in hopes of helping him. Peter ripped his jacket off himself and wrapped it around the man, trying desperately to smother the flames that engulfed him. Seconds seemed like minutes as he patted down the fire, but finally all the flames were extinguished. The professor lay on his back on the ground seriously burned. His arms were bent at the elbows as he held up his blackened hands. The look in his eyes was both shock and disbelief of what had just happened to him. He was shaking violently from the pain of his burns and the muffled sound of a scream remained caught in his throat. It reminded Peter of the hysterical hum of a massive beehive.

Peter knelt down beside him. He wanted to hold him, but was afraid of causing him more harm. Tyler stood beside them with tears streaming down her face and was mumbling over and over that they needed to get him some help. The professor reached out with charred fingers and grabbed Peter's shirt sleeve. He pulled him closer so that Peter could hear what he was about to say.

"Peter," he whispered feebly, "please ... give me... Last Rites." Tyler stopped mumbling and looked at Peter with her mouth agape.

"Please, Peter," the professor asked again.

"Jim, that was in another lifetime. You know that."

Tyler's mouth worked to form words, but there was no sound.

"Beggars ... can't be ... choosy. I ... don't see ... a ... line. Do you?" he struggled to say the words with blistered lips. "To me... Peter, you are still ... a priest." He closed his eyes.

"You're a priest?" She said.

Peter looked at Tyler. She stood staring at him. No doubt in shock over what she had just learned about him. He couldn't explain to her now. He would do that later. Right now, the professor had to come first.

"Tyler," Peter reached out and gently touched her forearm. "We need help, Tyler. Get help." He nodded at her over and over again until she nodded with him and he knew she understood what he was saying.

"Yes. Yes. I'll. . I'll get help." She turned, brushing back her hair with both hands, then started running out through the thick brush toward the ocean.

Peter watched her disappear into the darkness, then he dropped his gaze and granted his old friend's last request. As he said the final words and began to make the sign of the cross, he heard the professor exhale his last breath. A lump grew in Peter's throat and he leaned forward and buried his face against the blackened chest of his dear departed friend. He wanted to mourn the loss of a man that had become a father to him. To stop the madness before someone else died. But he knew the professor wouldn't want him to quit. He would want him to fight with everything he had. So he reached deep within himself and found the strength he needed to go on with the battle. He opened the front of the professor's charred coat and removed the coven's black book. In the distance he could hear Tyler's footsteps come to a halt. He could hear her call his name, but he couldn't answer. He knew she had sensed the professor's fate and had started back toward the stone shelter. Peter stood solemnly with the coven's book in his hand and walked to the shelter door.

"Peter!" Tyler yelled at him. He could hear the bushes snapping and cracking as she tore through them.

"Where are you going?"

He knew she could see him now.

"Come back! Are you crazy? Do you want to end up like him? Or my brother? Please, don't go in there! Don't do this to me. Don't do this to us."

Us. That made him stop in the doorway.

"What are you doing, Peter?"

"What we came here for," he answered. Then he walked into the darkness.

"Peter, no! Don't go in there. Please … come back," she cried.

He was out of her sight now, and he could hear her cry out for God to help them. He knew she had given up trying to stop him as he heard her footsteps fade in the distance and the rustle of the bushes as she thrashed her way through them to the water's edge.

Peter opened the trap door and went down the crudely made ladder and into the pit. The cellar was musty and smelled of dirt … and Gregory. His heart was in his throat as he thought of Gregory. He stood still and listened. Listened and prayed that he wouldn't hear Tyler's brother move as he had on his prior visit. It was quiet now. Thank God. He reached into the front pocket of his pants and pulled out a Zippo lighter. The cover clicked as he flipped back the lid, reminding him of the cocking of a gun, and suddenly he wished he *had* packed an Uzi in that duffle bag. He spun the wheel on the lighter and it sparked a flame that illuminated the entire dugout.

The room was larger than he had thought it was the first time he had been there, nearly twenty feet in diameter, he guessed. Mary Deven was nowhere to be seen. Gregory's body lay in a heap next to the dirt wall on the right side of the pit.

Across the room was a makeshift altar. It was, without a doubt, used for sacrifices, for Peter could see where blood had pooled on it and had turned black over the years. There was no time to waste. If he didn't stop Mary Deven now, the table might be used again. For him. He looked around the dugout, praying to find something to help him gain control of her. To somehow harness her power and use it against her. It would take more than bars of steel to hold her. This he knew. He would need a spiritual prison in which to contain her.

He reached into his pocket and removed the two fonts that the blind woman had given him. He held them, one in each hand, thinking how powerful the two liquids were that they would separate from each other if poured into the same container. Suddenly, he understood! Perhaps he had his prison right in his own two hands. He opened the font containing the oil and poured it on the floor, forming a circle about four feet in diameter. Then he opened the font of holy water and poured it out in a circle within the circle of oil. His heart pounding in his ears was still the only sound in the pit as he slipped his hand through the opening of his shirt and removed the coven's black book. He let out his breath and filled his lungs again before placing the black book in the center of the circle. He whispered, "For you, Professor Valkner, my dear departed friend, fire with fire."

Peter stepped as far away from the circle as the dugout would allow and waited in the darkness.

***

Tyler shivered as the cool breeze from the ocean

licked at the sweat on the back of her neck. Every muscle in her body strained to keep her legs pumping as she leapt from one rocky mound of seaweed to the next. A dark area loomed ahead of her and before she knew it she was airborne over the blackness. When she came down, it was hard against a barnacled rock. It tore her jeans and scraped her knee. She let out a cry of pain that was cut short as she came down with a thud, flat on her stomach. It knocked the air out of her lungs and she lay there with her mouth open wide, trying desperately to draw a breath. Panicking as one does in that painfully silent moment when the lungs are vacant of air, she turned over and lay there with her upper body propped against a rocky mound of seaweed. Her lower half lay in a puddle of salt water that had been left by the last high tide. While her belly still ached from the blow, she scrambled to her feet and tried once again to out run her fear, but it ran with her and whispered in her ear. It told her if she didn't get help soon, another would die, and then *it* would come for her.

She was running at full gait now, numb to the pain of her wounded knee. Her lungs had recovered from the painful blow and her panting mingled with the sloshing sound of the incoming tide. Suddenly her breath caught in her throat. She could see the pier! Never had a manmade construction looked so good to her. Hot tears ran down her face and she laughed. A single light halfway out on the pier illuminated a phone. It made her heart leap in her chest and filled her with hope that she could make a difference. It gave her the strength to press on, until at last she was rushing headlong out onto the pier, her feet only touching every fourth or fifth plank. She plunked her feet down heavily in an attempt to slow her stride as she neared the phone, but collided with it anyway. Her hands grasped for the phone and she felt it all over, as if she needed to prove to herself that it was real. Amazed that it was, and even more amazed that it hadn't been removed like most phones these days, made all but obsolete by cell phones. She grabbed at it with both hands and managed to get the receiver off the hook and placed it to her ear.

It was dead.

She whipped around and looked toward the village. It was as dead as the phone. The only light she could see was in the professor's kitchen. Again, a ray of hope. She left the receiver hanging by its cord and ran toward the light.

As she neared the door she prayed to God that Peter hadn't locked it. At first it wouldn't open, and she shook the knob with her right hand and pounded on the door with the other. She couldn't stop crying. All she could think of was Peter back at the stone shelter doing battle with the devil himself. She leaned forward against the door and began to sob, but was startled into silence when she heard the lock click. Slowly she turned the knob and the door swung open.

Adrenalin pumped in her veins again and she dashed into the kitchen. She stood in the center of the room and made a full circle, before remembering where the phone was. It was hanging on the wall next to the entrance to the living room.

"Oh God! Oh God! Oh God!" She bolted for the phone. "Please help me! Please help me," she repeated until her voice was just a whisper. She dialed "911", and paced back and forth in the wide archway between the kitchen and the living room, feeling like she was in limbo.

The phone rang and rang. When the operator finally answered, Tyler felt her heart leap in her chest.

"Please send help! One man has been burned terribly and the other is in great peril. Please hurry!" The words came so fast it didn't feel to her like she was the one saying them. She was connected to the sheriff and she gave him the details of where to send the paramedics. She could hear him telling her to stay put as she took the phone away from her ear and hung up. She couldn't stay put. She had to go back there. She had to help Peter.

Her head spun around, looking frantically for a weapon. There were knives in the kitchen, but she needed something more powerful. A gun. Turning on her heels she rushed into the living room. Even in the darkness her eyes caught movement and she froze in her tracks. She could see a small form standing across the room. She carefully reached for the light switch and flipped it on.

"Who are you?" she asked of a little blonde headed boy with freckles across his nose. "What are you doing here? How did you get in? Don't be afraid. I won't hurt you. Was it you that unlocked the door for me?"

The little boy smiled at her and bent down to the professor's suitcase and picked up his tape recorder with both hands. Tyler recognized it. It was the one the professor had brought to the séance. Her heart started pounding.

"Peter needs your help," he said calmly as he walked toward her. He held the tape machine in both hands, lifted it up, and held it out in front of her. "Take this to Peter."

Shaking, she took the recorder from the little boy.

He smiled at her and somehow he looked familiar. She shook the thought from her mind and told herself her imagination was working overtime. She closed her eyes for a second and tried to focus on the task at hand, and when she opened them again the little boy was gone! It was as if he had never been there. Except for one thing—she still held the tape recorder in her hands. A chill shot through her and she pulled the recorder to her chest and cried. It was all so overwhelming. So unbelievable. Yet, it was happening. She shuddered at the thought of what might be happening at the stone shelter and to Peter.

Peter! She had to get back to him. Now!

***

Peter stood flush with the wall of the pit. Waiting. The musty dirt odor of the dugout hung in his nostrils and he could taste the sour earth in his mouth. Just as he had for months after Daniel's death. It made him want to vomit. He closed his eyes and tried to push back the memories of that frightful day, and in that instant he heard the voice of the professor flood his mind like a rushing river, reminding him that Satan knows his weaknesses and will not hesitate to use them against him. Peter nodded as the voice of his departed friend schooled him as he had in life, and at first was calmed by the familiarity of it, then he heard a scuffing sound coming from across the pit. His breath caught in his throat. His eyes flashed open to see Mary Deven standing not more than fifteen feet away from him!

As she stood in the darkness of the dugout, she sniffed like an animal checking the integrity of its environment. Peter's muscles became as rock and he silently struggled to become part of the wall. Each time she sniffed, he gasped, wondering if it would be his last breath. She scuffed across the dirt floor toward Peter. His mouth was so dry he couldn't swallow. Surely she would kill him. His eyes clamped shut, not wanting to see his own fate, but then the scuffing stopped. He opened his eyes to see Mary standing just outside the circle. Her nostrils flared and the bridge of her nose wrinkled. Peter figured this was it. She would make her move on him now. Instead, she started to sing in an ungodly tongue that sent shivers down Peter's back. She sang softly at first, then louder and louder, as her decrepit body performed a dance around her sacred book that lay at her feet. Suddenly she stopped. She looked down at the circle that surrounded the book and then straight at Peter! A low growl that came from her throat told him she was angry that he had put a price on the book. If she wanted it, she had to enter the circle. Peter prayed her desire for the book was stronger than her need to kill him.

Mary's upper lip curled and she snarled at him as she stepped into the circle. She bent down and picked up the coven's sacred black book, pulled it to her chest and folded her arms over it. Peter let out a sigh of relief.

Mary laughed. "Dost thou think thou has the power to keep me here? You are not a captor. You are a murderer."

Though Peter knew it was a lie, the words cut deep into a wound that had never really healed. A lump formed in his throat and tears stung at his eyes. He could not let her do this to him.

"You are a liar, Demon!"

"Am I?" Mary closed her eyes and a black candle's wick ignited, casting a purple haze within the pit.

Peter smelled the pungent odor of cigarette smoke and heard a raspy laugh coming from the far side of the earthen room. He squinted and focused on the other side of the dwelling to see none other than Roberto Sanchez sitting slumped against the wall of the pit. He sat there puffing on a cigarette held between two yellowed, nicotine-stained fingers. He hawked up a clot of phlegm and spit on the circle. It spattered when it hit, spreading yellow, blood-streaked phlegm on the dirt floor. Peter watched it sizzle as it touched the holy water. Sanchez slowly opened his eyes and looked at Peter. They glowed a fluorescent yellow-green, absent of pupils. He dragged on his stubby non-filter cigarette and the smoke swirled up and around his face. He coughed and the accumulation of mucus and blood in his lungs rattled in his chest as he began to speak.

"You, Peter, *are* a murderer. Not once, but twice. And they are both here ... in hell ... with us."

"You are a liar!" Peter yelled at him. "Their souls belong to God. They are with Him." Peter felt sick and choked down the sour bile that burned at his nostrils and seared the walls of his throat.

"You are the liar! Not me," he told Peter. His gaze moved to the ceiling of the pit. "You *do* remember Michael."

Peter looked up. There he saw the little boy from that little town near Buffalo with his body pressed hard against the roof of the pit. Whimpers came from the little boy as drops of blood ran from his eyes.

"Why didn't you save me? Mother said you would help me," the little boy cried.

Tears rolled down Peter's cheeks as he fought

with the memories of that frightful night. "I did all I could, Michael. We all did–but it wasn't enough. You can rest now. God cradles your soul now, Michael."

"No!" he yelled, "I sit at the foot of the Beast and I have no peace. There's only pain here."

Roberto Sanchez began to laugh. "Only pain," he mocked the little boy, and laughed again. He wheezed as he spoke. "Now you believe me?"

"Never!" Peter struggled to remain steadfast in his belief that he hadn't failed that little boy so long ago, but as he listened to the sobs emanating from this juvenile form, his soul ached with sadness. Tears stung at his eyes and ran down his cheeks, and he could taste their salt in his mouth. His mind reeled with the images of the occurrences of that horrible night and he strived to oppress the overwhelming feeling of guilt. He clamped his eyes shut and tried to push the thoughts from his mind. His temples ached as his blood pressure continued to rise. His brain swelled with the memories and the sound of his heart pounding in his ears deafened him.

Mary stood in the circle with a smile on her lips. Her body swayed, as if in a trance, keeping time with a beat only she could hear. Then she began to speak with the voice of many demons, and across the room, Daniel appeared!

"Why, Peter? Why did you let me die? Why didn't you help me?" Daniel whimpered.

Peter stood in awe, staring at his little brother. He looked the same as he had on the day of his death; dressed in a pair of jeans with a hole in the right knee and a blue striped shirt. He stood on the lace of his left shoe. Peter was always telling him to tie the lace on that shoe.

A lump lodged in Peter's throat and he was unable to speak.

"You can help me now, Peter. Only you can set us free." He glanced up at Michael. "Please help us."

Peter bit his lip and wanted to close his eyes again, but he couldn't stop looking at his little brother. It had been so long. He wanted to go to him, snatch him up, and hug the life out of him. He loved him so much.

"Destroy the circle, Peter. It's all you have to do, and we will be free. *I* will be free."

Peter's body shook as he fought against Daniel's wishes. He could feel a force behind his heels trying to push him toward the circle. He whispered, "God help me. Give me strength to hold fast."

"NO!" Tyler screamed from the opening of the pit.

Mary looked up at her with wild eyes and hissed at her, spewing saliva from between her jagged teeth.

"Don't listen, Peter. Don't believe them," Tyler yelled down to him. "They aren't real. It's that witch. She's doing all of this. Don't listen!" she said as she fought against her fears of the closeness of the pit and made her way down the ladder to come to Peter's side. She held up the tape recorder, standing with her back to all of those in the pit, looking only at Peter. "Listen to this, Peter." She pushed the play button and the voice of Daniel filled the room.

It was a voice overflowing with love and it calmed Peter's soul like no sound he had ever heard. Daniel spoke of forgiveness and everlasting peace and the sound of his voice was like that of mighty rushing waters that washed over him and left a sweet scent on the wind that trailed in its wake. He looked into Tyler's eyes and saw reflected there the strength he possessed to turn the demons back to the hell from which they came. He took her by the arm and pushed her around behind him, and began to pray.

A deep growl came from deep within Sanchez, but soon turned to a gurgle as foaming bile came up out of his throat and ran down over his chin. His yellow eyes rolled up inside his head, leaving white orbs staring at the ceiling.

The malevolent entity that had appeared as Daniel began to convulse. Its feet rapidly pounded the dirt floor beneath it. Its mouth opened wide ... wider ... stretching yet wider, giving its face a grotesque Halloween mask effect. A scream came from within it, then the apparition disappeared with a shriek.

The image of Michael, with its back pushed hard against the ceiling of the pit, began to slither back and forth as if trying to find a way to escape. Finding none, it crept down the wall and crawled on its belly across the floor to where Mary stood in the center of the circle. It leaped toward her and grasped her around her lower legs. His mid-section came to rest on the circle of oil and holy water and at once its skin began to sizzle and blister. In an instant the image was no longer that of Michael, but was now showing its true self. It was a grotesque demon from Satan's own legion. Mary reached down and caressed the demon's head, then it, too, disappeared, leaving a scent of sulfur in the pit.

Mary's eyes flashed open and for a moment Peter saw fear in them. Then they were filled with anger and glowed with the fires of hell. A growl came from deep in her throat and the talons on the ends of her fingers pulsed with the anticipation of attack. She smiled at him with teeth that were jagged and black, and drool oozed from her mouth as she inched closer to the edge of the circle.

Peter began to pray a prayer that had been passed down through the ages. "In the name of the Father, the Son, and the Holy Spirit, I command thee, demon, to return to the hell from which you came. By the precious blood of the Lamb, He who is King of all heaven and earth, whose blood washes whiter than snow, I compel thee, old vile spirit, to be gone or to be cleansed!"

While Peter prayed, Mary screamed obscenities and cursed them and their God, her voice varying in tones of both male and female, until her voice was the sound of all the demons from hell. She tried to escape the circle, but could not step over the holy water. Every time her foot touched the edge of the barrier, her skin sizzled and she recoiled from it.

"I rebuke you, devil!" Peter shouted and held the Holy Bible high in the air. A pencil thin blue line flashed down from the Bible to the circle on the floor and it sparked when it hit the oil and flames shot up around the entire circle and surrounded Mary Deven.

She covered her ears with her clawed hands and cried out with pain as a huge welt appeared on her forehead in the shape of an inverted cross. Satan had branded her for all eternity. She crumpled to the floor and squirmed like a serpent as a green, foul-smelling bile ran from her mouth. Peter showed no mercy as he now prayed in tongues as the blind woman had done in the church. He didn't know from where the words came, only that they rolled off his tongue like the purest fountain.

Peter and Tyler then watched as the Beast appeared in the circle of flames. Its large, muscular body loomed over Mary, his faithful servant. It inhaled deeply with a force that pulled Mary to her feet. With its clawed hands it ripped the flesh from her body, transforming her into a bloody mass. Then the Beast opened its arms and wrapped them around her. A bloodcurdling cry came from her condemned soul as the Beast took her straight to hell. Peter and Tyler could hear the crackling flames and smell the brimstone of the everlasting fires of torment. Suddenly, Mary and the Beast were gone, and Peter and Tyler were left alone, in each other's arms.

In the darkness of the pit, two small forms appeared. It was Daniel and Michael. There was a sweetness about them and they glowed as they smiled at Peter and Tyler. Then their bodies became pillars of light as they ascended back to heaven. Peter cried with joy as he felt his burdens being lifted, and Tyler held him close and told him it was alright now. It was over.

They stayed in each other's arms until the rays of dawn filtered down through the opening above them, and lured them out of the pit. A sweet spirit filled the place, and as they walked out into the sunshine, they listened to the birds as they sang to the heavens. Not a word did they say as they passed the professor, walking arm in arm, leaving him, and Gregory, and the evil they had found there.

In the beginning God created the heaven and the earth. And the earth was without form, and void; and darkness was upon the face of the deep. And the spirit of God moved upon the waters. And God said, Let there be light: and there was light. And God saw the light, that it was good: and God divided the light from the darkness.

Genesis 1:1-4

CHAPTER 10–IN THE BEGINNING

It was a bright morning, despite the occasion. Peter thought that the professor would have liked it like this. Just a few friends gathering in a small country cemetery, saying their last goodbyes. There were more people standing around telling stories about him than there were people shedding tears. He would have liked that, too. Peter was sure that the professor, from somewhere better than here, was watching them and feeling good that he had brought a smile to their faces one last time. So for him, Peter fought the tears, then threw a bouquet of white roses across his casket as it was lowered in the grave. For the first time, since Daniel's death, Peter felt alone ... that is ... until he felt the hand on his shoulder.

"Are you okay?" It was Tyler. She was beautiful in

black. Her platinum blonde hair was as a halo in the sun's rays.

"I will be," he answered and patted the back of her hand that still rested on his shoulder. She looked at a taxi parked in the dirt courtyard between the small graveyard and the village church, then back at him. "You really have to leave now?" he asked her. "Can't you stay a while longer? I've made arrangements with Deke so that I can spend a few more days here. We could do some sight-seeing. What do you say?"

She smiled faintly. "Nah, I've got to get back to the magazine. Quite frankly, I've seen enough sights to last me a lifetime." She looked him straight in the eye. "I really do have to get back to New York."

Peter looked down. He wasn't sure if it was because he didn't want to see the hurt in her eyes that he had caused her, or if it was because he didn't want her to see the hurt in his that she was causing him by leaving.

"Someone has to make the arrangements for Gregory's ..." She couldn't finish saying the words.

"Let me help you with that. Please? Let me take that burden from you at least."

They found each other's eyes again, and Peter could see in them what she was thinking. That he most likely had handled a great many funerals ... as a priest.

"Will you at least give me a few minutes of your time before you leave? I need to explain," he told her.

"There's nothing you need to explain to me, Peter. I understand your choices, your dedication and devotion. I can't compete with that, it wouldn't be right for me to even try to."

He grabbed her by the elbow and pulled her to one side so as not to draw attention from the other mourners. He could feel the heat between them and wondered if she felt the burning, too.

"You've got to hear me out, Tyler. I'm not letting you go until you listen to what I have to say." He could see his own reflection in her eyes. He looked desperate to make her understand.

"Alright," she sighed, "I'll let you have your say, but then I have to leave."

"Let's sit in my car. Okay?" He backed away and held his hand out to her. He thought he saw her shiver just before she placed her shaky hand in his.

They walked back to his rental car and he opened the door for her to get in. She slid into the seat and he walked around the car and got behind the wheel. The car was well insulated from the sounds outside, and they sat there in silence, and watched car after car leave the burial grounds. The county sheriff was next to the last car to pull out. He slowed a little, peering through the passenger window at them, then shook his head and drove away. Peter knew the sheriff was uneasy with the explanation of what had occurred at the stone shelter, but he didn't have any evidence to detain them. Tyler watched him until he turned the corner and drove out of her view.

"You never told me what happened when you were questioned by the police. Did they believe you?" she asked.

"They believe what the medical examiner told them. I wasn't about to tell them what *really* happened. I've been that route before."

"What did the coroner say was the cause of their deaths?"

"They believe the professor was the victim of a rare case of human combustion."

"There are people that still believe that?"

Peter shrugged.

"And Greg?"

"An unfortunate fatal fall," he told her.

"How do they explain the wounds he suffered?" She grimaced and swallowed hard. Her eyes glistened with swelling tears.

"An animal, or several animals, they really don't know," he said quietly. She closed her eyes, no doubt trying to erase the image from her mind. Peter could have told her it wasn't going to be that easy, but he thought better of it.

"Well, maybe it is better that they don't know the whole story. I mean, who'd believe it anyway?" she remarked and forced a faint laugh. "I wouldn't have ... before this."

"The truth truly *is* stranger than fiction. They'd be chasing us around wielding butterfly nets, and promising us a new coat for the winter. One with extremely long sleeves that wrap around you and tie in the back," he replied so seriously. That made her laugh. He loved her laugh. It always made him want to laugh with her. And after all they had been through, it felt good.

"Tyler," Peter became sober, "I don't want you to leave."

"I have to. The magazine needs me."

"I need you."

"Peter…"

"Is that what you want? To go back to New York?" His eyes searched hers.

"It's not about what I want, Peter." She closed her eyes and shook her head, then opened her eyes slowly and looked at him. "You are …"

"Released," he blurted before she could finish her sentence. "I've been released from my vows."

"What?" She was stunned.

"I'm free, Tyler. Free of the priesthood, and held captive by you."

"Oh, please, Amado, you didn't just say that" She teased.

"Too, cliché? I'll work on it." He winked.

She laughed and shook her head, then became solemn again. He could tell she was confused and would need more of an explanation. He reached out and took her hand. She tensed, but Peter was encouraged that she didn't pull her hand away.

"When did this happen?" She asked.

"Soon after the professor and I left the debunking organization in Buffalo. The Church didn't take kindly to me disobeying their orders and performing exorcisms that weren't sanctioned by the Church. I was labeled a rogue priest, and asked to step down."

"Oh, Peter, how awful for you." Her hand now held tightly to his. "Surely you must have been devastated when they stripped you of your vows."

"Yes, I was. I didn't take my authority lightly."

"I'm sure you didn't. If there is one thing I am sure of, it's your dedication to what you believe in."

"Well, believe me, I certainly questioned myself more than once. I didn't feel much like a priest when I had to turn people away that truly needed my help."

"And so, you continued on your own?"

"With a little help from my friend, the professor."

"So you've been free to live–and to love–as any other man?"

"I've lived, yes, but I hadn't found love," he half whispered, "until now."

She looked at him solemnly and he could see her chest rise and fall with each breath as her lungs struggled to keep up with her increasing heart rate. Her voice, too, now a whisper as the words came directly from her heart. "You know, I think the first time I gazed into those vibrant blue eyes of yours, I fell in love with you," she smiled. "The chemistry between us was so strong. I knew you felt it, too. Then, I was so confused that night when you pulled away from me. I just couldn't understand why you did that. But now, I understand."

Peter nodded and sighed, then he swallowed hard. "In my mind, I still felt like a priest. The Church had released me, but my heart was trying so desperately to hold on to what it believed in. Sometimes, it takes true love to change a man's heart. That night, I think I panicked. I was so afraid that letting you into my heart would somehow destroy my faith, but now I know this is not the case. I've realized that my love for my creator and my love for you have already been co-existing. Love is a derivative from God. To reject it, would be a sin." He moved closer to her as the words flowed from his heart. He could feel her breath, hot against his skin, as she tilted her face up toward him and her lips parted slightly. He could stand it no longer. He kissed her passionately, feeling the hot unbridled love pass between them. When he finally removed his lips from hers, it wasn't because he was pulling away. Not this time. He only needed to look into her eyes once more to see his love reflecting in them. He would never pull away from her again, and he knew, looking into her very soul, that she wouldn't let him even if he tried. He belonged to her now, and she to him.

"Wait here," he told her as he got out of the car. He ran up to the taxi and spoke to the driver, then he rushed back to Tyler. He stood there smiling at her as he looked at her through the driver's side window. The taxi driver started the engine and drove away.

"Hey! Why did you send him away? I told you I have to get back to New York," she yelled to be heard through the closed window.

"A couple more days won't matter, will it?" he yelled back through the glass.

"Tell that to the magazine, Amado!" She shook her head and then smiled at him.

"If it's that important to you, I'll take you there myself. I'm not going to lose you, Tyler Moore. Not ever." Even through the closed window he could feel the heat radiating between them. As she smiled back at him, he could tell these were the words she really wanted to hear all along.

"Oh! I almost forgot," he said looking at her

through the window. "Wait here for just a second."

"Peter, where are you going?"

Peter hurried back to the one car that was still sitting in the cemetery, the Priest's car that had directed the burial service, and opened up the back door and reached in and pulled Phoenix out of the car with a leash. He led Phoenix back to his car and could see Tyler through the windshield. She was mouthing Phoenix's name, half laughing, half crying, but definitely happy to see him.

"We've got room for one more, don't we, Tyler?" Peter said as he opened the back door for Phoenix to hop in.

"Absolutely!" she answered. Peter couldn't tell who was happier, Phoenix or Tyler, but as he closed the back door he realized it was he that was the happiest of the three of them. And that truly made him smile.

Peter straightened before getting back into the car. He leaned against the side with his arms outstretched across the roof. He watched the priest who had performed the ceremony get into his car and drive away. In another lifetime, that would have been him driving back to the church. The priesthood had been good to him. He had learned a lot about himself. One of the most important lessons he had learned recently was that there was a time for every purpose under the heaven. A time to be born, and a time to die, a time to laugh, and a time to mourn, a time to hate, and now, a time to love.

He started to take his arms off the car top when he felt *the tug*. It was the strongest he'd ever felt, deep in his gut. It shocked him, paralyzing him in the moment of time, as he stared across the roof of the car and into a place within his own mind. The vision was at first out of focus, then as it became clearer his entire being shuddered to the core. He felt a tightening in his chest and his heart began to thud, pounding in his ears, drowning out Tyler's voice as her concerned cries for him faded into the distance.

***

The thunder of horses' hooves and the snap of twigs and boughs, broke the silence of midnight, and announced the arrival of Satan's faithful. The horses and their evil riders emerged from the shadows of the tall New England pines, and stomped into a field, glittering with crusty snow. Nervously, they pranced in place while their nostrils blew out clouds of vapor that hung eerily in the still air of the valley. In the center of them all sat the Beast upon his thrown and before him a figure robed in black knelt before him. A vile creature the size of a child slid off the back of a horse and came to sit at the side of the robed figure. Its long, sharp talons on the ends of its scrawny fingers pulsed with the anticipation of drawing fresh blood. An insane laugh escaped its throat as it reached up and pulled the hood from the robed figure and his gravelly voice bid her to look upon the Beast. The faithful applauded and the Beast threw back its horned head and roared. The vile creature, Cleobis, now clutched to his new mistress' leg as Sarah Deven accepted from the Beast–the legacy of the Evil Reign.

About the Author

***

Kaelin C. Murphy was born and raised in Maine, and grew up hearing stories passed down from generation to generation about ghosts, hauntings, demons, and witchcraft. Her family's strong, spiritual beliefs were instilled in her at an early age, defining the lines between good and evil. Though she later moved from the state of Maine, her roots still run deep in the legends that refuse to stay buried.

She was co-editor of The Center Post, a bi-monthly local newspaper back in the 1970's and since then has published several poems in various anthologies. She enjoys watercolor painting, wood working, playing various stringed instruments, fishing, and of course, writing. She is a graduate of The Institute of Children's Literature.

She now lives just south of Atlanta, Georgia.